THE TRIUMPH OF LOVE AND LIBERTY

By the same author

The Dragon and the Needle, Book Guild Publishing, 2014

THE TRIUMPH OF LOVE AND LIBERTY

Hugh Franks

Book Guild Publishing
Sussex, England

First published in Great Britain in 2015 by
The Book Guild Ltd
The Werks
45 Church Road
Hove, BN3 2BE

Copyright © Hugh Franks 2015

The right of Hugh Franks to be identified as the author
of this work has been asserted by him in accordance with the
Copyright, Designs and Patents Act 1988.

All rights reserved. No part of this publication may be reproduced,
transmitted, or stored in a retrieval system, in any form or by any
means, without permission in writing from the publisher, nor be
otherwise circulated in any form of binding or cover other than
that in which it is published and without a similar condition being
imposed on the subsequent purchaser.

All characters in this publication are fictitious and any resemblance
to real people, alive or dead, is purely coincidental.

Typesetting in Sabon by
Keyboard Services, Luton, Bedfordshire

Printed in Great Britain by
CPI Group (UK) Ltd, Croydon, CR0 4YY

A catalogue record for this book is available from
The British Library.

ISBN 978 1 910298 69 5

To Stuart Watson

Chapter One

Paul Johnston's life began on 20 March 1920 in a house on Richmond Hill. His mother had been a very unhappy woman for the nine months it had taken to bring Paul into the world – neither she nor her husband had wanted any children.

The Johnstons had met while taking cover in a Zeppelin raid on London during the war. She was a nurse, he a successful stockbroker. It was a cosy shelter – a shop doorway near Liverpool Street Station. They had stood next to each other and it had seemed the most natural thing in the world for him to put a protective arm around the waist of a pretty little nurse.

Johnston, too old at fifty-five for active service, was still young enough at heart to meet his nurse the next day, and by the end of the following week he proposed marriage. She was nearly twenty-two. He explained, 'My first wife never really understood me – she knew I didn't want children but because I wouldn't let her have any, she left me.'

'Where is she now?'

'Somewhere in America – she met a Yankee in London. I believe they have six children now – these new nations need large birth rates – she's obviously helping them very well.'

She laughed, liked him, and then fell in love. She loved him even more when she had seen his house on Richmond Hill. And because she had hated the poverty of her parents in Sheffield, she readily agreed not to have children.

An ex-nurse should have known about these things, but after that birthday dinner the previous summer, when she had

had too much to drink, she had forgotten about taking 'precautions'...

Paul began to realise that he wasn't wanted by his parents somewhere near the age of six. The previous year they had moved from Richmond to the coast at Brighton. Mr Johnston was well able to afford one of the large Regency houses near the boundary with Hove.

Brighton in the late 1920s was a happy place for children, with a quiet and safe beach, where at low tide a little boy could forget his unhappiness at home among the rocks, or netting for shrimps on the sands. In the early days there was no one to disturb him down there on the beach. And Paul used to enjoy sneaking through the turnstiles on the pier when the attendant wasn't looking. And then at the end of the pier, he would watch the men fishing.

But it was on the beaches where his education began. He started meeting other boys and girls – mainly boys. Most of them came from the slum area of the town. By the age of ten, Paul had grown into a handsome lad and had become a leader of one of the gangs the boys used to create on the beaches. And create they did!

Paul's mother knew nothing about this. She was more interested in caring for her Regency house than she was in caring for the boy. Her husband was equally indifferent, for he was much too busy making money at the Exchange. However, on Sundays they both did what they considered the main duty of parents. Paul was taken by them both to church in the morning, and in the afternoon a car was hired and a picnic tea arranged to be eaten on one of the highest points on the Downs.

It came as a great surprise and shock when one afternoon in early summer, a policeman rang the bell of the Johnstons' house.

'Yes, what's the trouble?' Mrs Johnston asked him, in the way people always assume trouble when the Law calls.

'Mrs Johnston?' he inquired.

She nodded.

'Do you have a boy called Paul?'

'Yes, has something happened?' she asked in an anxious voice.

'Now don't you worry too much – may I come in for a moment?'

'Yes of course.'

On the way to the lounge she asked again if something had happened to Paul, for he had been out since lunchtime and it was now five o'clock. This normally would not worry her at all. As he sat down the policeman asked if Paul would be home soon and said that, as far as he knew, nothing had happened to the boy.

'Yes, he should be home any time now,' she said.

'Well, madam,' continued the policeman, 'this afternoon, during what we suppose was some good-natured fun on the beach, a little girl had a bucket thrown at her. Luckily it just missed her eye, but it gave her a nasty cut on the side of her head and I have reason to believe that the bucket was thrown by your little boy. The mother is naturally in a state about it. She came to us soon after it occurred.'

'What a dreadful thing to happen!' She paused. 'How do you know that Paul threw the bucket?'

'Oh, we don't think there's much doubt that he threw it – you see, the girl's mother was there when it happened and we knew it would be him from the description she gave us.'

Mrs Johnston was horrified. 'You talk as if Paul has had previous trouble – I just don't know what you are talking about!'

'As a matter of fact we were coming to see you about him anyway, but this particular thing has forced our hand. I patrol the beaches during the daytime and for some time now I have noticed that your boy is often making a nuisance of himself – it was only the other morning that he was having a stone fight with some other boys.'

At that moment the front door opened. 'Come into the lounge, Paul,' shouted his mother. She knew if must be him.

'Coming, Mummy, I'll just wash my hands first.'

'No, come in here immediately.'

As Paul entered the room the policeman stood up. Paul stopped when he saw him.

Mrs Johnston frowned. 'This officer tells me that you threw a bucket at a little girl this afternoon – now tell him it isn't true.'

Paul said nothing.

'Well, Paul, I'm waiting – did you or didn't you?'

'Yes, I did,' he suddenly blurted out.

'Oh Paul – how *could* you?' whispered his mother.

'Quite easy, Mummy, you just pick it up and throw.'

'Now look here my boy,' cut in the policeman, 'what you did could have resulted in serious injury and—'

'What does serious mean?' asked Paul.

'Serious means dangerous – the bucket only just missed the girl's eye.'

'Why did you do it?' Paul's mother asked.

''Cos she threw a stone at me first and it only just missed my eye.'

'That may be so,' sympathised the officer, 'but two wrongs don't make a right. In any case, I was telling your mother that you are often in fights on the beach.'

The officer's voice droned on, while little Paul thought how unfair the world was, to allow a girl to throw stones and not get into trouble and yet, when he fought back, *he* did. The policeman was just finishing and Paul heard him say, 'So I will leave the boy to you, Mrs Johnston, but I hope that his father will deal with him.'

When the policeman left, Paul started to say 'I'm sorry, Mummy, but it really was her fault and—'

His mother cut across his words with the order that he should go to his room and stay there until his father came home.

Later that day the world seemed even more unfair to young Paul for, on his return from the City, his father, on hearing the news, immediately went to his son's room and gave him a thrashing.

Chapter Two

The headmaster of Paul's preparatory school called himself Doctor John William Jason. He had no academic right to the title 'doctor' – it was self imposed – but he had, over a period of many years, built a solid reputation in successfully getting the boys through the public school Common Entrance Examination. He was more like a prosperous businessman than a headmaster. The fees were high and he was able to attract first-class staff. His gown had been bought by his wife at a second-hand clothes shop near the Lanes in Brighton. She was as thin as he was fat – they made an odd-looking couple.

Doctor Jason was a great believer in the use of the cane. He knew of the existence of Paul's school gang, for Paul, as well as having the beach gang, had readily formed another with his school friends. But its exploits seemed harmless enough – they only appeared to consist of the cowboy-and-Indian type of game after school hours on the playing field. He knew nothing of the gang's pursuits on their way home, until the arrival at the school one morning of an angry Mrs Hicks. She ran a sweet shop near the school. She complained bitterly about the behaviour of a group of boys both outside and inside her shop.

'It has been brought to my notice,' said Doctor Jason sternly at the school assembly after lunch, 'that certain boys, in addition to having satchel fights outside Mrs Hicks' shop, have also indulged in appalling behaviour inside the shop as well. Now will the boys responsible please stand up?'

For a moment or so there was no upward movement from anyone, but then quite suddenly Paul got to his feet.

'Come to my study immediately,' said the Doctor to Paul. 'The rest of you will go to your classrooms.'

With encouraging jostles from his friends, Paul made his way to the Head's study. 'Now come and stand here by my desk, Johnston.' He frowned heavily at the boy. 'Before I administer the punishment you so richly deserve, I want to know where a boy of your age learned to use a particularly bad word. I commend the way in which you so readily came forward at assembly, but Mrs Hicks also told me that you had called her a...' he paused, 'a bloody old cow.'

Paul tittered.

'How dare you treat this as a laughing matter!' boomed the Head. Paul went very red in the face. 'Do you realise that I can send you home immediately with instructions that you are never to return?'

This had two effects on the young Paul – the first was one of an inward pleasure at not going to school, the second one being outward dismay at losing the gang he had trained so well.

'Oh no, sir,' gasped Paul. 'Is that what Mrs Hicks said I said?'

'It was as she said.'

'Then I must have said it, sir.'

'I cannot believe that you heard that word at home, and as for here at school, that of course is quite out of the question. Now, where did you hear that word coupled with such a very rude description of Mrs Hicks?'

'Sir,' explained Paul, 'I heard it used many times on the beach by people who seemed angry, and I was angry with Mrs Hicks so I used it too, and ... I heard you use it the other day.' A dreadful silence followed.

'Bend over, boy.' The boy of not quite ten years then received six very painful strokes on his buttocks. At the end of the beating, his left hand went swiftly to the seat of the doctor's pants, where a large and painful pinch was administered.

'Out! Home!' thundered the head. 'You are expelled! Out! Home! Get out, collect your things – out, home!'

The head carried on repeating 'Out! Home!' as Paul made for the door, which he swiftly closed behind him. He ran quickly to the changing room, collected his satchel and sped to his classroom, where Mr Brett was trying to drum into the heads of very disinterested boys the rudiments of elementary French.

'Now, translate the following from the board: *voilà la porte, la table, le livre. Où est le livre? Le livre est sur la table...*' At that moment 'la porte' was thrown open by Paul, and before a startled Mr Brett could do anything, Paul shouted, 'I have been expelled – see you later!'

As Paul ran down the driveway of the school, he began to wonder what his next move should be. To go home, he supposed, and yet he was afraid to face his mother – even more to face his father. He decided to go to the only place where he might feel secure – the beach. At two o'clock on a summer afternoon he found that place too hot – his school uniform also made him conspicuous. By half past two he had made his way home. His mother was out, and having no key, he decided to return to the seafront. He left his satchel under the seat of a covered front shelter and made his way to the largest of the two piers, the Palace.

Chapter Three

In the 1920s and early 1930s, before Hitler's rise to power, an Anglo-German society had been formed, composed of ex-servicemen from the two countries. It had little chance of success, for the events of the next decade were foreseen by so very few. It was a pathetic, though well-meaning, attempt by some of the men who had faced each other in the mud of Flanders to create a fraternity and, through their friendships, express to the world the hope that the Great War truly was the 'war to end wars'. They hoped to achieve this by a series of exchange visits to each other's countries and thereby establish mutual understanding and confidence.

On the afternoon of 15 July 1931, as Paul was approaching the Palace Pier, a German steamer was tying up at the end. Aboard her were many hundreds of Germans, members of the Anglo-German society, on their way to visit the English members in Brighton. They were to tour the town during the afternoon, and later that evening, to be the guests of the mayor at a banquet in the town hall. As Paul sneaked through the turnstiles without paying, the reception committee was escorting the Germans out of the pier onto the front.

Paul wandered to the pier's end and, leaning over the railings, looked down at the German ship below. 'I would like to go on that boat,' he said to himself – and that is exactly what he did! No one noticed the little boy going down the gangplank. Then he saw some stairs going down below the deck. He went down them and at the end of a long corridor he noticed an open door. He made for it and, on entering the cabin, he saw in its far corner a heap of blankets on which he lay down and immediately fell asleep...

The leader of the German party visiting Brighton, Erik Heide, was a man in his late fifties who, towards the end of the war, had commanded a battalion on the Somme sector. He had lost his only son in the early part of the war, and his wife in the flu epidemic which had swept through Europe after the war. He was now a successful import/export agent in Hamburg. He had a fluent command of English and his tall, erect figure commanded respect from his English friends. His speech of thanks at the end of the dinner in the town hall was brilliant, not only for its faultless English, but also for its candour.

After thanking his hosts for the entertaining afternoon they had had, he continued: 'Only thirteen or so years ago we faced each other as foes in a bitter and bloody war. Tonight we face each other as friends in the hope that never again will the world be plunged into so terrible a conflict. My office in Hamburg is a five-minute walk from my home. To get to it I walk across our public gardens, thinking what an easy target this open city would be for a bomber. The contrast between the lake and the beautiful flower beds, for which our gardens are famous, and the towering trees planted so long ago...' He paused. 'The contrast between this peaceful picture and what the place might look like after hundreds of bombers had done their work has this effect upon me. It makes me realise how much I love peace, how much I love life and how much I want to remain an individual. I have been bombed many times and each time my respect for the individual is considerably increased. It is the individual that carries the hopes of the future, and not governments. If we always remember that as we go about our tasks in our own countries, we may yet establish a peaceful era, stretching for generations ahead.'

As Heide sat down amid fervent applause, a mile away Mr Johnston returned from his fifth search of the beaches, to find his wife making her twentieth phone call to the police. When Paul had failed to return home by six o'clock she was not overly worried, but when at seven, on her husband's return from the City, Paul had still not come home, she phoned the school.

'Your boy was expelled by me this afternoon,' said Dr Jason. Then he gave an exact account of what had occurred, by which time Mrs Johnston, distracted with worry, was lost for words, and it was only when Mr Johnston took the phone from her that the problem of the boy's whereabouts was rationally discussed.

Dr Jason assured Mr Johnston that he was only doing what he thought was best for the school and said that the boy, no doubt, was on the beach and would soon come home with his tail between his legs. He hoped, in any case, that the Johnstons would be more careful in future in their choice of language. Jason firmly replaced his receiver, and Mr Johnston did likewise.

'What are we going to do with the boy?' cried Paul's mother.

'I have had a particularly bad day in the City,' groaned her husband. 'I suggest that in future you exercise a much greater control over him and, for a start, forbid him to go anywhere near the beach. Then you must make him understand—'

'I have so much to do,' she cut in. 'If you knew how much extra work there is in this house, and you spent more time spending money instead of making it, and being a proper father to Paul—'

'And where is the boy now?' broke in her husband. 'I'll go down to the beach, and when I find him, he's going to get it.' Off went Mr Johnston, and as soon as he had gone, his wife made another call to the police.

Chapter Four

The German ship came from Bremerhaven and was due to leave Brighton Pier at 11 p.m. Herr Heide led the party back to the ship, and they went aboard, standing on her upper deck shouting their farewells to their hosts, while a band played the national anthems of both countries. They all stayed on deck as the ship cruised about half a mile offshore, and they were able to follow the flashing car lights of their friends, who kept up with the boat as far as Seaford. Then, as the ship steered further out to sea, the coastline receded and the passengers made for the bars below.

It was nearly two o'clock before Heide finally went to his cabin. Paul had been asleep for twelve hours. The steward had not returned to the cabin to prepare the bunk, as he had been ashore. Heide discovered that his bunk was unmade and was about to ring for the steward when he suddenly noticed Paul. He went over to him and gently touched his shoulder.

Paul awoke. 'Where am I?'

'You, my young man, are on a ship, and you are in my cabin!'

'Well, I must go home, because this afternoon I was sent home from school – Mummy and Daddy will be very cross with me, so I don't really want to go back.'

As an afterthought, he said, 'I'm hungry.'

'Where do you live?'

'At Regency Terrace.'

'In Brighton I suppose?' said Heide.

'Yes. I'm hungry,' Paul repeated.

THE TRIUMPH OF LOVE AND LIBERTY

Heide helped the boy to his feet. His first impulse was to ring for the steward, but he didn't – instead he said, 'What is your name?'

'Paul. What's yours?'

'Herr Heide, er Mr Heide.'

'What a funny name – but I like your face.'

Heide grinned. 'This situation is not very funny though, is it Paul? At the moment you are many miles away from Brighton with little hope of getting back there for some days. You are on your way to my country called Germany. The first thing we must do is to tell the captain about you and get you some food, then try and get a message to your parents. They will be very worried about you.'

'No, they won't,' answered Paul. 'I don't think that they really like me very much. You see, I'm always getting into trouble and .... I'm hungry,' he broke off.

'Well, let's see if we can find you some food.' He took Paul by the hand, and the two made their way to the forward saloon. Some of Heide's friends were still in there and they looked up with astonishment at the pair as they entered.

While the men talked to each other in German, Paul looked around, liking everything he saw. The ship was riding a small swell, and as she gently rolled he started to run back and forth with the motion. He was fascinated by the paintings of ships on the walls, and climbing onto a chair he looked out through a porthole. In the distance he could see the lights of another ship, and quite close by, the flashing lights of a buoy.

'Now Paul,' said Heide behind him, 'come and have some food; then we must see what we can do with you.' The boy started to eat the strange-looking food in front of him. He immediately liked the long sausages, was not too happy about the bread, but approved of the hot chocolate. All the time he was eating he was surrounded by the group of Germans. Heide was perturbed by the lad's lack of feeling for his parents. Far from feeling homesick, he seemed to be thoroughly enjoying himself.

Heide and the others agreed that to call the captain so late at night was unnecessary, and in any case there was little that could be done before the morning. The steward had been called and the arrangements made for Paul to spend the night on the spare bunk in Heide's cabin. Before Heide left the saloon with Paul, he had made arrangements for a cable to be sent, telling Paul's parents of the lad's safety.

The next morning the Johnstons got the message about Paul. Neither had had much sleep; they were as much worried about what people would think as they were for Paul's safety.

'How are we going to get him back?' moaned Mrs Johnston.

'I haven't the slightest idea,' said her husband, 'but I know one thing – I'll give him the hiding of his life when he is back! Of all things, there he is with a crowd of bloody Germans.' During the war Mr Johnston had contributed nothing to its successful conclusion and had in fact made a considerable sum of money. His only inconvenience had been the lack of notepaper, and the nearest he had come to action was the Zeppelin raid on London, during which he made a mental note to buy shares in companies that would be rebuilding the damage.

By the time Paul had gone ashore at Bremerhaven, he and Heide had become great friends. Trips to the engine room had been mixed with visits to the bridge. The ship's captain had allowed Paul to sit at his table. He was spoiled by them all. The German police came aboard as soon as the ship docked, and after a long discussion with Heide, it was agreed that he should look after Paul until the necessary arrangements had been made to send him home.

THE TRIUMPH OF LOVE AND LIBERTY

Heide's home in the suburbs of Hamburg was an imposing place. Built by his father at the turn of the century, it was a big Gothic-style house managed by his housekeeper, Frau Wendt, a large, motherly type of woman. As soon as Heide told her of Paul's adventure she immediately grasped him in a close embrace. His little head was lost for a while between her vast breasts. She could not speak a word of English, but her affectionate mutterings and clutching gave Paul his first sensations of what warmth truly meant.

'How long will he be with us?' she asked Herr Heide.

'Some days, I imagine. It will be quite like old times, Hilda, eh?'

'When I was nanny to your son, I had my happiest days,' she said. 'He's a fine-looking boy.'

Please – what are you talking about?' asked Paul.

'Why, we are saying that you look like my son. Hilda looked after him when he was a little boy,' Heide said. 'He was very brave and was killed during the war.'

'How was he killed?' asked Paul.

'He was in the Army, and one day he was leading his men into an attack – he was hit by a bullet, Paul, and killed.' He paused, 'Wars are bad things, for at the end of them no one is really the winner.'

'When I fight on the beach,' grinned Paul, 'I always win. It's because my gang's tough – tougher than the others. I like fighting, so if you are the winner you must be better.'

'No, Paul, life is not quite like that, as you will find out one day.' Heide continued, 'Love for other people is the really strong force in the world – those you like and those you dislike as well. Your parents, now, they love you.'

'No they don't. Mummy doesn't like me, nor does Daddy, and I hate them! They don't love me at all!'

Heide gave Hilda a modified version of what Paul had said, for he had no desire to worry the old nanny. Paul went over to the window and looked out onto the beautiful garden.

He thought how super it would be to live here, and although there was no beach, he had noticed the very large river in the city. He liked Heide and Hilda. They were kind to him. He decided he wanted to stay here with them always.

Chapter Five

At the inquest the train driver was blamed, though he, poor man, was dead too. For some unknown reason he had missed the red for danger signal – his train had crashed into the stationary suburban train at Croydon. The trains had reared up in the air and, at the point of impact, formed an enormous V over the rails. All the occupants of the first coach were killed, among them Mr and Mrs Johnston, on their way to Hamburg via Tilbury Docks to collect Paul.

It took two days for the news to reach Herr Heide. Paul had become very difficult since being told that his parents were on their way to collect him. He had been staying with Heide for ten days now. The British consul at Hamburg had been helpful. It was he who told Heide of the sudden death of Paul's parents. 'Can you come to my office as soon as possible?' he had said to him on the phone.

'So you see, Herr Heide,' added the consul later in his office, 'the boy has no relations in England – there is an uncle on his father's side who lives in Canada – he might take Paul.'

But Heide had already had a long talk with Hilda and was eager to adopt the boy. He said as much to the consul.

'I wouldn't know about that,' he answered. 'Paul has inherited quite a considerable sum of money. There will be that to settle and no doubt many other problems as well. I'll give you the solicitor's address in London and I suggest you contact them.'

* * *

'Hilda, where's Paul?' Heide asked on his return.

'He's in the garden. Herr Heide, are we going to be able to keep him? He's such a pleasant boy and I can't understand why his parents were so cold with him. He's already made friends with the two Ritter boys from next door. You should see them playing together; the language problem doesn't seem to exist. Paul already seems to be the leader too!'

'I don't know yet,' replied Heide. 'There are many problems to resolve.' He told her of Paul's relations in Canada and of his legacy. 'We shall see, send him in to me, please, Hilda.'

As Paul entered the room he could see from Heide's face that his parents were liable to arrive very soon now.

'Yes, Mr Heide,' the boy said. 'I suppose they're nearly here.'

'Paul...' he stopped. He couldn't find the words. He only knew that he mustn't tell the boy the full truth just yet. 'Paul,' he continued, 'your mother and father had an accident in England, while on their way to collect you, so you see they will not be here just yet – they have got to get better first. It may be some time before they arrive and in the meantime you are going to stay here with Hilda and myself – do you want to do that?'

'Oh yes, of course I do – I hope they never come for me! I love it here and I think you and Hilda are super. I already have a gang with Ernst and Hans as my men, and tomorrow Hilda says that she is going to take us to the public gardens to play and perhaps go on the boats on the lake.'

For a moment Heide pondered on whether to tell Paul the truth. But instead he said, 'All right, Paul, off you go to the garden and play.'

Ernst and Hans were waiting. The three boys then ran to the end of the garden. Waving his arms in the air and pointing to the top of the large fir tree, Paul started to climb it, followed by the two German boys. Heide was watching from the window.

THE TRIUMPH OF LOVE AND LIBERTY

It took nearly a year for Heide to complete the legal adoption of Paul. During this time Paul attended a day school in the centre of Hamburg. Heide made many journeys to London to see the Johnstons' solicitors. He was able to combine his business affairs with these trips. Paul's relations in Canada were indifferent to the problem, which made Heide's task easier, for the boy's solicitors had felt from their first meeting with him that Paul would have bright prospects in such a man's care.

Paul was told of his parents' death two weeks before his first Christmas in Hamburg. 'Paul do you like it here still?' Heide had said to him.

'Very much, Mr Heide,' the boy had replied.

'Would you want to stay here always?'

'Oh yes please,' Paul had answered. 'I like the school you have sent me to and I can already speak quite a lot of German, and the masters like to hear me speak English – it's fun.'

'You have never asked about your parents.'

'No.'

'Why not, Paul?'

'Because I don't think about them very much.'

'Paul, in August, when I told you that they had had an accident, that wasn't exactly so...' He hesitated. 'They were both killed in a train crash on their way to collect you.' He went on quickly, 'We want you to stay here forever with us. But you have an uncle in Canada, and you might be able to go there if you wanted.'

'No, no. I want to stay here,' Paul said. 'I'm sorry to hear about Mummy and Daddy.' This was the nearest the boy got to showing any emotion.

Heide did not tell him about his inheritance.

When he had recently been in London, the solicitors had told him that when the estate was finally settled there would be in the region of £25,000 for Paul. The final figure would depend on the amount obtained for the house in Brighton. The money would be kept in trust for him until he was twenty-one years of age.

It was on Christmas day 1931 that Heide told Paul that in future he was to call him Uncle. Paul never mentioned his parents in front of Heide or Hilda again.

Chapter Six

In October 1932, Paul's adoption by Heide was completed. On his previous visit to London in August, Heide had met the General Secretary of the British Legion. At this meeting the arrangements were made for the members of the Anglo-German Society to visit Hamburg the following spring. Heide told the secretary about Paul. 'What an excellent opportunity to encourage better relations between our two countries,' the secretary had said.

'Why yes – I had not really considered that. The boy is still a British national,' Heide said. 'It worries me sometimes to think that since 1863 the history of my country has been marked by wars of aggression. I like to feel that I am now a peaceful businessman.'

'And why not?' the secretary replied. 'The thought of another war is surely enough to keep the peace – all the major powers are now disarming, and once the world's trade recession has been defeated, all should be well.'

'It is difficult for my country...' Heide hesitated. 'There was so much bitterness after the last war. Remember, we were the losers. There is emptiness in our country at present, there is much sadness too. I hope for a good man to lead us, but it is difficult to see one. Hindenburg is too old.'

'I saw that a man called Hitler was Hindenburg's rival at your presidential elections last April. What's he like?'

'I know little about him. He seems to make a lot of noise in the Munich area. He's certainly a change from the run of Prussian officers – I believe he was a corporal in the last war. I cannot believe that he could be the right man. I think that the most successful leaders generally have a good educational background. They have had their minds trained to consider and attempt a rational approach to their countries' problems.'

'I think that the men who fight the wars should have a much bigger say in fighting for peace,' urged the secretary. 'It seems to me that this may be the one safe way of keeping peace. By the way, that speech you gave in Brighton last year was given wide publicity in our more responsible newspapers.'

'I had heard that. I meant every word I said. Dreadful errors can be found in the histories of every civilisation. We must all try and learn from each other.'

'I often reflect,' replied the secretary, 'that one of the most remarkable circumstances in our two countries is the way in which our two royal families should be so inter-related, and yet go to war with each other.'

'I often think that too – could it be that so far we have had the worst of the bargains? We've had the black sheep of the family and you've had the white.' He laughed.

'No,' Heide replied, 'that's over-simplifying the whole problem. But I firmly believe that the economic problems and instability of Germany and her previous states is the matter that should give you the most concern.'

'Yes, you are probably right. As you know, I lost two boys in the war, and I know you lost your only son – so let us work for peace, for them, and for our future.'

Later that day Heide had gone to keep a business appointment in the City. The import agency Hodges and Thomas, run by the former and lived on by the latter, had benefited greatly from its association with Heide. This was one of those rare occasions when Thomas decided to appear in person at the office. It was he who met Heide in reception. But Thomas had not closed Hodge's door sufficiently, and Heide heard Hodges say, 'The bloody German is outside...'

* * *

THE TRIUMPH OF LOVE AND LIBERTY

Paul did well at his Hamburg school, and by the time that Hitler gained his absolute majority in the Reichstag, young Paul had become leader of his class. He was thirteen. In the winter of the same year, 'Uncle Heide' took him and the Ritter boys for a skiing holiday in the Hartz mountains. It was during this holiday that the three boys had their first contact with the Hitler Youth Movement. Staying at the same hotel was a young man, Fritz Balke. A good skier, he spent many mornings with the boys, teaching them the elementary principles of the sport. In the evenings after dinner, while Herr Heide played chess with a friend in a far corner of the lounge, Fritz would tell the boys of the joys of belonging to the Youth Movement. He described the summer camps, the organised hikes and marches, the games and the skiing camps. The boys liked Fritz more and more.

Paul had a room to himself. The fourth night, he had just turned his bedside light out when there was a knock at his door. He got out of bed and, standing by the door, asked who was there.

'It's me,' said Fritz. 'I would like to come in for a few minutes.'

Paul opened the door. While he closed it, Fritz made his way to the bed and lay down on it.

'Come over here, Paul.' The boy sat down.

'I like you more than Ernst and Hans,' whispered Fritz. 'I like you very much; come and lie by my side. Take your dressing gown off first.'

'Why?' asked Paul. 'I'm cold.'

'Take it off and lie by me, I'll keep you warm.'

Paul took his dressing gown off and lay down beside Fritz.

'You're a nice boy, Paul.' Fritz put his arms around the boy's shoulders. 'Would you like me to do some nice things to you,' he continued, 'like this?'

Paul had once seen two boys embracing each other in a quiet corner of the gardens in Hamburg. When he and the

Ritter boys had talked about it they had laughed – but now he did not know what to do about what Fritz was doing to him. He wanted to tell him to stop, and yet he didn't.

Fritz lived in Hanover. He was orphaned by the war and lived in the city with his aged grandfather. It was during his period of training as a bank clerk that he had his first contact with the Nazis. Within a short time he had become the leader of the first Hitler Youth Movement, formed in secret by an older member of the Party.

His perverted mind was given ample outlets for his sexual experiments. He was the cause of tragic consequences in the lives of many young men. But in the cruel and oppressive years that lay ahead, this merely became one of thousands of corruptions that affected the lives of so many people.

His influence on Paul was immediate and it initiated him into the world of the Nazi Party. The two kept up a regular correspondence with each other, and in the following year they both went to a Youth Summer Camp on Luneburg Heath, some twenty miles south of Hamburg.

When Heide had been told by Paul about the camp it led to a strained conversation between the two. Heide was very worried by the boy's apparent fever of excitement about the holiday.

'Paul, I am far from happy about this idea.'

'What idea, Uncle?' replied Paul. 'The idea of a camp?'

'Not so much the camp as your interest in going with Fritz, who is quite a few years older than you, and your enthusiasm for the Party. I haven't told you yet, but I am also far from happy with the people who now rule us, and I am by no means alone with this thought.'

'Fritz is a very good friend to me, and as for the Youth Movement, its main idea is to bring young people together. It also emphasises games and encourages us to keep fit – surely that's good for us?'

'Paul, I do not like the way the Nazis are gaining power – they have already caused much unnecessary suffering to many Germans. If Hindenburg should die, then Hitler will have supreme power which he has virtually got already. His treatment of the Jews has already resulted in our country losing some of its best brains – they are just being hounded out of the country. I am afraid that this Youth Movement has been created by the Party for purely political reasons – to teach the young the importance of the Party. The individual will count for nothing.'

'I am not in that position, Uncle. I am not even a German subject yet. I am just known as "Paul Heide" and no one seems to realise that I am still a British subject. It's just what I imagine the Boy Scouts are like in England. We don't discuss politics at all.'

'That will come, my boy. I have recently been giving serious thought to sending you back to England – at any rate to a school there. I think the time has come to tell you that at the age of twenty-one you will inherit a large sum of money from your father's estate. In a nutshell, Paul, I do not like the way this country is going; I fear for its future. It's not the country I had hoped would develop from the results of the last war and therefore, as I am responsible for your future, I have been giving serious thought to what I consider is the best solution for you.'

'But I am so happy here! And now I can speak both English and German. How can there be any serious trouble? You often say that another war is impossible. Only the other day you said that the Anglo-German Society is making good progress.'

'It's difficult to describe how I feel about the future of this country, Paul. I am not sure that I know anyway. But something bad is developing.'

'I don't want to leave this country! Hilda certainly won't want me to go – but of course, if you do not want me – I suppose I will have to understand.'

'You know that I don't want to send you away!' cried Heide. He sighed. 'You may go, this time,' Heide continued reluctantly, 'but after the camp next month we must have further talks.'

It was now July 1934. The following month, Field Marshal Paul von Hindenburg died and Adolf Hitler then exercised supreme and uncontrolled authority with the only legal political party in the Reich – the Nazis.

Chapter Seven

While Paul attended the six-week Youth Movement Camp at Luneburg, Heide went on one of his business visits to London. He was able to meet many of his contacts in the Anglo-German Society at a cocktail party being held at the London section. It was at this party that he met Colonel Henry Bedford, who was serving in the intelligence branch of the British Army. On receiving a regular commission in 1918, Bedford had remained in the services and now, at the age of thirty-eight, had been appointed controller of the department concerned with Germany. It was not by accident that he was introduced to Heide.

'And how goes the German side of the society?' had been Bedford's opening remark after meeting Heide.

Heide grinned in reply. 'My own side in Hamburg is thriving, and we have many members who are becoming very pro-British. How long that is able to continue, unfortunately, may be open to doubt.'

'Do you have doubts about the continuity of goodwill toward us, Herr Heide?'

'Oh, I didn't quite mean that. I'm sure there will always be plenty of goodwill towards your country. It's just that I feel apprehensive about the future. There are some disagreeable trends in our land at the moment.'

Such as?' cut in Bedford.

'Well, to take just one example, the Nazi Party is very anti-Jewish and this group of people is beginning to suffer such indignities that many are leaving the country. We have a dictatorship – this could be good for people if it was based on the right principles. Sadly, this is not so, and I fear trouble cannot be far away.'

'I don't agree, Herr Heide,' Bedford goaded him. 'Hitler has stated that he has no desire to cause trouble either in your country or in the world. He wants to put your country on its feet and in the process is bound to hurt many feelings but, in the long run, it may all be for the best.'

'I don't mind people's feelings being hurt,' explained Heide, 'but I do mind when their basic freedoms are taken away.' The conversation ceased while a waiter refilled their glasses. As the waiter moved away, Heide went on, 'I have been giving very serious thought to leaving the country myself.'

'Isn't that deserting the ship when it's sinking?' asked Bedford. 'Surely Hitler needs all the help he can get, especially from such as you? Perhaps that's a bit strong – I apologise if it is.'

'No need to apologise. The situation for me is not cut and dried. I have adopted an English boy – I have to think of him too.' Heide then briefly told the colonel about Paul.

'I think you were most generous to take him into your home, Herr Heide – and you say that he likes living in Germany?'

'Very much – it is a good place for young people to live in at the moment – and that's not contradicting what I have been saying! Youth is very important to the Nazis – appealing to the young. It helped to get them into power, and young people will get preferential treatment. You'll see that happening – the older generations will be put out to grass.' Heide laughed. 'I only hope, Colonel, that the grass is green and that we have plenty to eat!'

'Is Paul going to finish his education in Germany or will you send him to one of our boarding schools?'

'I am not sure yet what I will finally do. But if I do send him to England, which school would you recommend?'

'Without a doubt, mine. Let me know if you decide to send him there.'

'That is very kind of you, I'll certainly remember that.'

Paul was enjoying his camp.

It had started badly, for Fritz had said embarrassing things about them both in front of other boys and there had been lots of laughter. Paul had run back to his tent, but Fritz had followed and the damage to their friendship was quickly repaired.

By the end of the first week Paul had been taught how to live off the land, how to build a raft to cross small rivers, and how to give first aid, and he had learned the words of patriotic songs sung round the campfires in the evenings. As it was a mixed camp, he also learned that kissing and cuddling a girl was more fun than whatever it was between him and Fritz.

Anna Stucklen was a pretty girl who looked older than her fifteen years. She had perfect features; her blonde hair was long, but she had discovered a knack of tying the long tresses around the top and side of her head. This had the effect of making her look taller than she really was. Her ample, firm young breasts completed an almost perfect Aryan type. Her eyes were a deep blue. Paul and Anna sat next to each other during the political lectures that started towards the end of the week.

These were given by a senior Nazi and took place every morning for the remainder of the camp. Between the 'Heil Hitler' salutes which marked the opening and closing of the talks, the young people were infused with the glories which awaited them from the benefits they would all obtain from National Socialism. The Führer was embarking on a programme of expansion from which the Fatherland would one day not only regain the territories it had lost in the last war, but would also spread its authority throughout the world. Such were the long-term objects of their illustrious leader. He would demand absolute acceptance of his orders, for only in this way could his will be done. It was the duty of all the German people to increase the population as rapidly as possible. Young people would, whether married or not, produce children. The state would take over at birth and be responsible for their upbringing. It was also the duty of all true Hitler Youth members to report on any traitors in their midst. Traitors were people who in any way criticised the leader or any of his ministers – even relatives would not be excluded from this ruling. Every true young Nazi would loathe and despise the 'Jewish swine' who had been responsible for Germany losing the war. Action was already being taken to rid the country of these pests ... and so on, every day of the camp.

By the last night of the camp, most of the boys and girls had fornicated. Paul and Anna were not the exception. Already attracted to each other, what else could their young bodies do but – to use the excuse of the camp leader's encouragement – indulge in what was after all a very pleasant pastime! Anna had already slept with many boys, so Paul's inexperience and shyness was quickly overcome by her.

He left the camp with a certificate of efficiency – a much older boy than his years, and with a complete adoration and worship of Hitler and his Party.

He also managed to retain his friendship with Fritz. When Paul had told him that he enjoyed relationships with women, Fritz confessed that he had also developed a love for girls as well.

Chapter Eight

The telephone in Heide's bedroom had rung six times. On the seventh he answered it.

'Herr Heide?' a voice said.

'Speaking.'

'In fifteen minutes' time, two men will appear at your front door. We do not want any fuss, so you will be there and admit them.'

'Who is that speaking?' demanded Heide. 'What on earth are you talking about?'

'Never mind who it is speaking. Do as you are told and there won't be any trouble,' the voice persisted.

'Now look here!' shouted Heide. 'I don't know who or what you are, but in fifteen minutes' time there will also be some police at the door, so your friends will get a double welcome, from them as well as myself.'

'That will be a complete waste of time, Herr Heide – this is the Chief of Police speaking. If you try to ring the police in the next fifteen minutes, you will find that they will not answer – much better that you employ the time preparing to meet these men.' The phone went dead.

Heide wondered if he was he having a bad nightmare. The phone was still in his hand. For a moment he sat on the edge of the bed staring at the phone. He stood up, walked to the dressing table, then to the wardrobe and back to the dressing table, then to the wardrobe and back to the phone. 'Give me the police, quickly, operator,' he said.

'Hold the line please.'

He looked at his watch. It was 2.30 a.m.

'Hello operator, hello operator...' he moved the hook rapidly up and down.

'Hello sir, there doesn't appear to be an answer.'

'That's absurd, there must be.'

'I agree, sir, it is most unusual.'

'No, it doesn't matter,' said Heide.

'Is there anything wrong?' The operator had detected the anxiety in his voice.

'Yes, I had a mysterious phone call a few minutes ago – some men are coming to see me. Will you please go on trying to get the police? You have my number.' He gave the operator his address. Heide continued, 'Tell them that I suspect robbery or something, I don't know, but tell them there is obviously trouble of some sort on the way for me. I won't open the door until they arrive – tell them that.'

'Yes, of course, sir, and you had better be careful,' the operator said. 'In any case, I will phone you again in about ten minutes or so – my name is Lucke, Gerhard Lucke.'

'Thank you very much, operator.' Heide put down the phone. He was confused and troubled. It was now 2.38 a.m.

He put on his dressing gown and went to the door of his room. Paul was standing outside. He had returned from camp a few hours earlier.

'What's wrong, Uncle? I heard you on the phone.'

Heide told him of the call and then said, 'Go back to bed, Paul, I expect it is only a hoax.'

'No, I will come downstairs with you, Uncle.'

'No, you will not. Now get back to bed.'

Paul made off to his room, but as Heide descended the stairs Paul returned to the landing and stayed hidden in its shadows.

A few minutes later he heard the doorbell ring and he saw his uncle move towards it. 'Who is there?'

'It's the police, please open the door.'

'How do I know it is the police?'

Something dropped through the letterbox.

Heide picked up a police identity card. He opened the door. There were two men, one in uniform, the other in civilian clothes wearing a heavy black leather coat.

'What do you want at this time of night?' asked Heide.

'You had the phone call, Herr Heide?' said the plain-clothed man, and, pushing passed Heide, he entered the hall, closely followed by the officer, who then firmly shut the door. This done, he then said they had some important questions to ask him.

'Then we will go to my study.'

Paul could hear no more, so he returned to his room.

'We apologise for getting you up at this hour,' went on the officer once they were in Heide's study. They had sat down. Heide stood behind his desk, leaning on his chair. He was still bewildered, although now completely awake.

The plainclothes man, who introduced himself as Seebohm, spoke.

'Herr Heide, it is better that we see you here and not at your office. It is also better that we see you at this hour and not at a more civilised time.'

'That is a matter of opinion,' cut in Heide. 'I think it's scandalous to subject me to any questioning at this hour. I am of course ready to help the police in any matter in which I can be of any help. However, at the moment I am not only sleepy, I am also a very angry man – but go on, what are your questions?'

'Herr Heide,' continued Seebohm, 'we know that you make frequent journeys to London for business reasons.' Heide nodded. 'We also know that during these visits you have many contacts with British people, especially with the Anglo-German Society members. That is so?'

'Of course,' Heide confirmed.

'We also know that on a recent visit you met a Colonel Bedford at a cocktail party in the capital.'

'Yes, I did.'

'That is good to get your confirmation.'

'And what is good about that?' said Heide. 'It just happens to be the truth.'

'It is good that you have confirmed it, for it shows that you are truthful.'

Heide struck in with, 'That is something I always try to practise, and as I cannot see where this conversation is getting us, I suggest you get rapidly to the reason for your visit.'

'Indeed, and as you always tell the truth, it is good to know that we will get confirmation of the facts we have on your talk with Colonel Bedford.' Seebohm's tone of voice hardened. 'And now here is the reason for our visit. You have made derogatory remarks about the Fatherland to Colonel Bedford.' His speech quickened. 'You also indulged in treacherous, disloyal and complete fabrications about our leader and his Party. This is so?'

Heide was baffled. He was certain that no one had overheard his conversation with Bedford. What did it matter anyway? Perhaps this was all a wild dream?

He said, 'Since when has it become unlawful to express one's views?'

'You don't deny, then, that these things were said?'

'I object to misinterpretations being put on a private conversation – *private*, mark you!'

'There were many other Germans present,' Seebohm put in. 'We depend on getting a good name abroad for our party from people such as you, Herr Heide; you will be more careful in future no doubt.'

'Is this all you wanted to say?' enquired Heide.

'Yes, for the moment. But in future, you will be watched very carefully. It would be a pity, not only for you, but also for your business, if your permit to travel abroad was withdrawn. Remember, this can be done. We feel sure, however, that from such a man as you, with a fine record of service to Germany to your credit, that no further warnings will be necessary. Don't bother to see us out, Herr Heide. Good night – or rather, good morning.'

Heide had stood all the time. When the two men had gone, he picked up the phone and called the operator again. 'Is that Herr Lucke?' he asked.

'No, sir.'

'Could I speak to him, please? It's about a call I made a short time ago.'

'Hold the line please.' Then, a moment later, 'I am sorry, sir, we have no one of that name working on our switchboard.'

'But you must have – he told me his name was Lucke – er, Herr Gerhard Lucke.'

'I am sorry, sir, you must be mistaken.'

'But,' contradicted Heide, 'he was going to—' He paused. 'Oh, never mind, operator.'

Heide returned to his room. He saw the sun rise over the city of Hamburg – it was going to be a beautiful day.

At breakfast, Paul asked his uncle who the men were, and Hilda asked what they had wanted at such an hour of the night.

Oh, it was a private matter concerning a customer of mine,' Heide had replied.

'Uncle, did you get all the postcards I sent you on the last day but one from Luneburg? I had such a wonderful time that I thought I would try and write a different story on each one. Oh, and thanks for all the letters you sent me. Here's a pipe for you, and Hilda, a gypsy skirt for you – how's that for a dutiful boy?'

They both gave the boy their thanks and he continued, 'You know, Uncle, Hitler is a wonderful man and Germany is very fortunate to have him as their leader. There are some marvellous years ahead for us all.'

When Heide got to his office he immediately wrote a letter in his own hand to Colonel Bedford. Two days later all his private and business post was opened at the Hamburg Gestapo Headquarters. His letter to Colonel Bedford was the last one to escape these searches.

Chapter Nine

Heide could tell that the letter from Colonel Bedford had been opened before it was delivered to him – somebody had made a careless job in re-gumming the label.

> *Dear Herr Heide*
> *I am very pleased to know that you have decided to send Paul to this country to complete his education. He is, of course, a little beyond the usual age of entry but I am certain that if I have a word with the Headmaster the boy should be able to gain admittance for next Easter Term; but you will have to move quickly. Perhaps you could let me have your final decision by return?*
> Yours truly
Bedford

Heide had got to make up his mind about Paul's future – he had told no one of the visit from the police. He couldn't discuss the problem with any of his friends, but he could talk to Hilda. He took Colonel Bedford's letter home with him that evening.

'Has Paul come home yet?' he asked as Hilda opened the front door to him.

'No, not yet, Herr Heide.'

'Hilda, I have something very important to discuss with you this evening – it's about Paul.'

His hurried speech and manner worried Hilda.

'He's not in any trouble is he?' Hilda asked in an anxious voice.

'No, should he be?'

Hilda entered the study with him. 'No, Herr Heide, but now we are talking about the boy, I have been thinking that there's something about him that is a bit different. I was going to speak to you about it, and also about some papers and photos I found in the bottom of his wardrobe.'

'I see. Well, let us get that over first. As he might come in while we are talking, I suggest that we have a chat in my study this evening after he has gone to bed.'

'It goes back to the time he met Fritz,' explained Hilda, ignoring what Heide had just said. 'You haven't seen too much of him in the past few months, but since he met Fritz he will not go to church with me any more.'

'Hilda, why on earth didn't you tell me at the time?'

'I am sorry, Herr Heide, but I didn't want to worry you and I thought he would change his mind and come with me. I don't think that you have looked in his room recently – he's got a large photo of Herr Hitler on the wall, and then this morning in the wardrobe I found some horrible things that the boy has written about Jews in a scrap pad, and on the back cover detestable photos, photos of women with no clothes on. I have left them there.'

'I don't know what to say, Hilda – you were right to leave these untouched. Now look, don't say anything about this to Paul. See me in here late this evening, and I will decide what's to be done.' At that moment the front door opened.

'Evening all,' shouted Paul. He appeared at the study doorway.

'Hello Paul,' said Hilda.

'Must go up to my room 'til supper – see you then.' He ran up the stairs two at a time.

'Hilda,' murmured Heide, 'I shall speak to Paul after supper about what you have said. From the way he behaved just now I can see how out of touch I am with the boy. I shan't say you made the discoveries – I'll say that I did, so you must pretend that you know nothing. It is better that way. I don't imagine he will talk to you, so try not to worry, and come along here when Paul has gone to bed.'

Hilda nodded, went to the door, paused, then returned to Heide and said, 'I don't know what's happening these days to young people. We do our best to bring them up in Christian ways and they don't seem to take any notice of our teachings. I wonder where we're going wrong, and I wonder if it's the same in other countries?'

'I don't know either – I don't know either,' Heide repeated. His eyes looked very tragic as he wondered how he was going to handle this problem.

During the meal Paul suddenly said, 'Uncle, can I ask Fritz here for Christmas?'

Heide looked at Hilda. He said, 'I'm not sure about that just now, Paul.'

'But Uncle,' continued the boy, 'he's done lots of things to help me and he's so very generous. There's a very good chance that I will be made a section leader in the Youth Movement we have at school now, and if I am, it will be entirely due to the training Fritz gave me at the camp.'

'I can't give you a definite answer now, Paul. In any case, it will give extra work for Hilda, and we must ask her.'

'I'm sure she'll agree – won't you, Hilda?'

Hilda said she was sure she didn't know.

'Paul, I want to have a chat with you after supper,' Heide said, 'so come along to my study, will you?'

'Yes, Uncle. It won't take long, will it, because I have some writing work to do in my room?'

'I don't know how long we will be, Paul, just come along. In fact, we might as well go now. The boy followed him sullenly.

'You sit over there,' Heide said pointing to his red leather armchair. 'Now Paul, make yourself comfortable because this may take some time. It is certainly going to decide how your next few years are going to be spent and where they'll be spent. I'll come straight to the point. I am going to send you to a school in England – it's a boarding school in the south and not very far from Brighton, so you'll be able to renew your English friendships. The school is called St Peter's, Elthorne. It's a very well known public school.'

The boy looked at Heide with astonishment and said, 'But why, Uncle? You know how happy I am in Hamburg – all my friends are German – I haven't got any English ones. I don't want to go to England.'

'Look, Paul, you won't be in England all the year – all your holidays will be spent here, and that will be three months of the year.'

'But what about the Youth Movement? I am German now.'

'You're not naturalised yet.'

'No, but I belong to Germany now. I believe in the Nazi Party! Its aims are the right ones for young people. I might as well tell you, Uncle, that I have every intention of making it my career.' The boy's eyes lit up with excitement, and he started a long sermon based on all he had been taught about the Party.

'Don't talk to me like a pamphlet,' Heide broke in angrily. 'You know nothing of the basic problems which face this country, and nor do the Nazis. It's a party which will fail because it has no concern for the individual, and it's even more doomed to failure because it is anti-Christ.'

'How can you speak like that about the man and party who are dedicated to the task of clearing up the mess left by your generation? And as for the Jews—' He got no further.

'You will not speak to me like that – what you have said has finally determined me to send you to England. I have also seen the contents of your wardrobe, Paul.'

Heide stared at the boy. Paul stared back. Then he lowered

his face and said, 'It's not fair to look at my things, and—' He faltered. 'I am a bit mixed up about that.'

'Paul, can't you see that perhaps it's the people you have met and the way of life they have been talking about that may have caused these problems for you? When I took you into my home it was because you needed someone to look after you and take care of you; at the moment I feel that I have failed in that task.'

The boy's expression was peculiar – not exactly hostile, but certainly not friendly. Heide went to the window and stood looking out. He felt very angry. He went back to his chair and sat down, suddenly extremely tired. He looked at the floor and frowned heavily. Damn Hitler! Damn the Nazis! He looked up and found Paul staring at him.

'I'm sorry, Uncle,' the boy said humbly.

'Well,' Heide smiled and looked at Paul steadily.

'I'll go to – what's the school called?' Paul asked.

'St Peter's, St Peter's, Elthorne.' They shook hands.

Later, when Heide told Hilda, she seemed very pleased.

Chapter Ten

On 21 January 1935, the train in which Paul had travelled from Victoria station stopped at Elthorne station. It was a cold afternoon and the morning's frost had not thawed from the rooftops. As he opened the carriage door he saw on the notice in front of him 'Elthorne (alight here for St Peter's College)'.

He stepped out onto the cold platform and, passing through the barrier, saw a taxi at the station entrance. He was a day late in arriving; heavy gales in the North Sea had delayed the boat from Hamburg by twenty-four hours.

The taxi driver lowered his window and, still sitting in his seat, said, 'You for the school, lad?'

'Yes please.'

Paul got in the car. It moved off in a series of wild jerks – the engine coughed, spluttered and then decided to propel the car forward at a very slow pace.

'You're a day late, lad.'

'Yes – I have come from Germany and my boat was delayed by rough weather.'

'Never mind, that's one day less of term for you. You're new, aren't you?'

'Yes. What's it like?'

'The school, you mean? Well it's been here well over a hundred years and the boys always look happy – yes, it's a good place I should think.'

They drove on in silence. 'This is College Lane. You'll see the school round the next corner.'

St Peter's was built of Sussex flint and stood in about

twenty acres of its own grounds. Founded for the furtherance of Christian education for the sons of the clergy and the upper middle classes, it was of imposing architecture in the French Gothic style. Paul's first sight of the school on this cold winter's day did little to make him feel happy!

Through the taxi window he saw first the high chapel tower and then the wide spread of the buildings around it. The place looked cold and forbidding. He could see no sign of human activity. The taxi swung into the wide gravel entrance, passed a large house (which he later discovered was the Headmaster's) and then pulled into the outer quadrangle. Viewed from the air, the main school buildings formed a large letter 'H', the top of the 'H' being the inner quadrangle, and the bottom part the outer. The taxi stopped in front of the porter's lodge, and it was then he saw the first sign of life. Out of the lodge entrance came a little man wearing a blue-and-white striped jacket, grey flannel trousers and a toothless smile.

'Good luck, lad,' said the taxi driver. 'You'll soon find your feet.'

'You're a bit late,' said the porter. 'Follow me. What's your name, boy?'

Paul told him.

He followed the porter through the lodge entrance, at the end of which two long monastic cloisters branched to the left and right. Turning left, Paul saw window seats on his right which looked out onto the inner quadrangle, and to the left, large oak doors spaced about ten yards from each other. The porter stopped in front of one.

'Your house master's in here. What's your name again?'

'Heide, Paul Heide.'

The boy saw on the door 'M.W. Mott, MA (Cantab)'.

'Master "Hider", sir,' said the porter on opening the door. Paul was then half pushed into the room.

'Good afternoon, Heide. When you did not arrive last night, we phoned the shipping office and they told us of the delay.'

Mr Mott had been at St Peter's for thirty five years, twenty-five as a house master. His dress was still Edwardian, his philosophy Victorian. He was dedicated to his work, unmarried and, as is often the case with bachelors, always in the right. Paul looked at the master's face. Outwardly, it was kindly and intelligent – but he would soon discover that behind that face lay hardness.

'Yes, sir, I am sorry—'
'You speak English quite well.'
'I am English.'
'Yes, of course. The headmaster will want to see you later – in the meantime I welcome you to St Peter's. You did well in the entrance papers. The boys are still in class. I think it best for you to go to the school noticeboard and spend a while reading the various rules – the ones applying to the school in general and the others to your house in particular. The captain of your house is called Roberts – you would not normally have much contact with him for some days, but in view of the unusual nature of your start as a new boy, I considered it best for him to have some quiet words with you before meeting the others.'

'Yes, I see, sir. Shall I go to the noticeboard now?'
'Please.' Motts went to the door with Paul. 'At the end of this cloister, turn left and you will see the board immediately on your right. I will arrange for Roberts to meet you there.'

It was so quiet everywhere, Paul thought. So different to Hamburg. The board was a mass of information. No running in the cloisters. Call-over at 6.30 a.m., 4.30 p.m. Tuck shop opening hours, lights out – great lists of instructions. An interesting one caught the boy's attention: 'While school maids are in the wardrobe, no boys are to enter.' The fact that girls were about made life seem much more promising – the 'wardrobe' puzzled him though.

He heard in the distance a high, light-pitched continuous sound. The rolling noise grew closer and suddenly it was upon him. The voices of hundreds of talking boys. They were pushing and jostling each other, walking in groups of twos, threes and more, though occasionally a lone, sad-faced boy would rush past.

Suddenly Paul received a very painful blow on his bottom. He turned his five-foot-ten body and faced a youth of similar height.

'What the hell do you think you're doing standing there with your hands in your pockets?' said the kicker. 'Oh, you're new,' he continued, and turned to walk away, but not far. Paul had been well taught in self-defence by the Youth Movement. He swung the side of his right hand onto the nape of his attacker's neck. The boy crumpled, falling on the hard concrete, where he lay motionless. Within seconds a large group of boys clustered round.

'Here comes Mr Davies,' said a young voice.

The group suddenly disappeared and Paul was alone. 'What has happened here?' said a small, frightened man. The master's gown was so long it nearly touched the ground.

'This boy kicked me so I hit him back,' said Paul. Davies bent down, and the boy made a grunting sound and, with the master's assistance, sat up.

'What's your name?' asked Davies.

'Heide, sir, Paul Heide.'

'I see – you're new?'

'Yes.'

'You say "Yes, *sir*",' said another voice – it was Paul's house captain, Roberts.

Paul turned to face Roberts. The fallen boy was now on his feet, rubbing his neck.

'Roberts, take over this new boy,' stuttered Davies, and then turned to Paul's victim. 'Are you all right now?'

'Yes, thank you, sir.'

'You will report this to Mr Motts, Roberts,' Davies muttered and walked away, thankful that the fallen boy seemed OK.

As Paul later discovered, Roberts was captain of the school as well as his house captain. He was a natural leader.

'That was a pretty good start to your life here,' Roberts said to Paul. To the other boy he said, 'What happened, Osborn?'

'He was standing there with his hands in his pockets so I rousted him – and then he hit me behind the neck.'

OK, Osborne, off you go. Heide, follow me.'

And so it was that within half an hour of his new life, Paul found himself trailing behind the school's captain.

On the way to Roberts' study, Paul was intrigued to notice how boys moved aside on Roberts' appearance. Groups of boys who were on the way to their house rooms made a clear path for him, even those who had their backs to him.

Paul and Roberts entered a small room furnished with three armchairs and a large desk. In one corner there was a small table which was laid for tea, in the other a large gramophone. On the top of this was a pair of rugby boots. There was a bookcase covering most of one wall. On the wall facing the door were three rows of school team photos, underneath four canes of varying length. It was a room Paul would soon know well.

Roberts sat in an armchair; he was a handsome boy resembling his famous film-actor father.

'Heide, that boy you knocked down is what is known here as a school prefect. He has a perfect right to kick in the backside any boy who is found breaking the school rules. I know you come from Germany, but Mr Motts told me that you can speak English. Therefore, you understand me so far?'

'Yes, I do, sir ... that is...'

'Don't call me sir – you call masters sir – you call all boys by their surnames. Go on.'

Paul continued, 'That is, I assume the word *backside* refers to the behind.'

Roberts continued, 'The rule you were breaking was that

of having your hands in your trouser pockets – only school prefects can do that, and school colours – you'll understand who they are in a few days' time. Because of your age you will be sleeping in the senior dormitory and using the senior houseroom. There is every likelihood that because of this you will become cocky – that means too big for your boots – and you've made a shocking start. Unless you're very careful, the next few weeks will be very unpleasant. Roberts broke off and looked at Paul, who proceeded to stare back at him.

'It's usual for new boys when they first arrive to have these things explained to them en masse. I'm going to give you a week to find your feet and in a moment will call in a boy called Jenkins – he's not a prefect, but he's known as the senior boy of the house room. He has orders to guide you by the hand for a few days. If you listen to him carefully and do what he says, you'll be all right. If you don't, then you will only have yourself to blame for an unhappy time here.'

Roberts got up, went to his door, and let out an ear-splitting cry of, 'Boy!' Within seconds, one appeared who was told to fetch Jenkins immediately. Roberts waited at the door until a very spotty-faced youth appeared. This lad was introduced to Heide. 'Off you go then,' said Roberts, and as Paul reached the door, he went on, 'Oh by the way, Heide, when a senior boy looks at you, don't stare back; if you do, he'll tell you to "switch off" – this means look away from him. If you don't, you'll get a beating.'

Paul wandered off in the direction of the senior house room with the boy Jenkins. He was sure that Uncle Heide would strongly disapprove of the rough treatment given to individuals, and as for his much-loved freedom of speech! Ah well!

Chapter Eleven

It was Paul's fifteenth birthday – and the prediction of his house captain, Roberts, had proved painfully true for him. He had been beaten for various petty offences once a week for the first two months. He had earned a reputation for toughness and the way in which he stood up to older boys had won the admiration of many of the younger ones. Paul had gained the friendship of one of these smaller fry, John Bright. The lad had a curious-shaped face, a very turned-up nose and small, deep-set eyes. He would have been ugly but for an extremely intelligent expression that made his face interesting.

The two boys had also developed a sexual attraction for each other, and whenever the opportunity arose, Paul encouraged and led John into the ways of male love.

Paul also discovered that the 'wardrobe' where the maids sometimes worked was in fact a large room in the upper cloister where the girls went each afternoon to repair boys' clothing. Most of these young women came from a poor area in North Shields and were chosen more for their industry than for their beauty. Sometimes, however, a pretty one would get through the net of the matron. Such a one was Ruth. In addition to repairing clothing, the maids' other duties were serving in the dining hall and making the boys' beds – and Paul seized the first opportunity to date Ruth. Teatime gave him his best chance as no masters were present at this meal.

'Ruth,' Paul had said to her one day during tea when the term was only two weeks old, 'how about meeting me behind the gym tonight?'

'Eee, you booger,' flowed her north-country accent, 'ye knows I can't.'
'Why not?'
''Cos if I'm caught I'd get sacked.'
At least she hadn't said no, thought Paul.
'We won't get caught, Ruth. Come on, be a sport!'
Three days later she agreed to meet him. The timing was most important. There was only half an hour available between supper, which finished at 7.30 p.m. and prep in the house room at 8.00 p.m. It had been snowing, and at least a foot of snow lay in the yard behind the gymnasium.
'Hello Ruth,' Paul whispered as he pulled her into the protection of an arch which acted as a buttress to the gym's wall. 'And look, call me Paul.'
'Ee, Paul, it's cold,' she complained, and then, 'I can't stay long.'
'Well, neither can I, so let's get down to it.'
'Get down to what?'
'Well, to this of course!'
Anna had shown Paul many of the finer points in making love, but without a girl of experience he was still somewhat lost. As an excited little boy might be on his birthday, tearing eagerly at the paper wrapping hiding a present, so Paul started to take apart Ruth's clothing.
'Here, stop that, lad!'
'What do you mean, stop? What do you think we're here for?'
'Not that.'
'Now don't be silly, Ruth, it's nice.'
'Now don't be bloody daft, lad, this is not the time or place for that.'
'It's all right, Ruth, look!'
She saw that Paul had a wax candle in his hand.
'And what do you think you're going to do with that? Eee, you booger!'

Ruth hurled herself from his grip and ran off towards the school buildings, stumbling in the snow, then getting up and finally escaping into the school. She need not have run so fast, for Paul made no effort to follow her. Instead he leaned against the gymnasium wall and laughed.

John Bright knew of Paul's obscene little plan. He was waiting for Paul on his return to the house room.

'How did it go, Paul?'

'Oh fine, just fine, John,' he said and followed with a full description of the meeting with Ruth, until a prefect told them to stop talking and get down to their prep.

Paul wrote every Sunday afternoon to Heide. He received a reply every following Wednesday. His first letters were full of woe, and upset his uncle. But as Paul settled down to the routine of public-school life so his letters became more cheerful. Heide was pleased to notice that the boy made no reference to the Youth Movement or to Hitler. Heide was not due to make a business trip to England until the early summer, so arrangements had been made for Colonel Bedford to take the boy out at half-term.

The colonel had duly arrived and taken Paul to Brighton, after Sunday morning chapel. They had gone to see his late parents' house, then on to the Palace Pier, where the boy gave the colonel a full description of how and why he had smuggled himself aboard Heide's ship many years before. Bedford was impressed with the boy's frankness and liked the lad more as the afternoon wore on, and he found it difficult to understand why Mr Motts had taken him aside after the morning service and said that although Paul had settled down, in some respects he was still extremely worried about the boy's behaviour. For his first term they had decided to make great allowances for his obvious difficulties in getting used to the school's way of life. But the constant need to beat him for varying offences made Mr Motts wonder if the boy would ever settle down.

In any event, Paul had come to like his first term – he

particularly liked his introduction to rugby football, his friendship with John Bright, his little bit of fun with Ruth and the ease with which he took to his classroom work. He also realised that in the following term he would have to settle more into the discipline of the school if he was going to carry out his instructions and orders from the Nazi Party in Hamburg, delivered to him via the Youth Movement. It was vital for him to stay at the school for at least three years, and his complete adoration of the Führer held him steady for the long-term object. It was difficult at times to avoid any reference to what was going on in Germany, and very tempting to make some mention of it to his friend Bright.

When the holidays came Heide met Paul off the boat at the Hamburg Docks.

'Paul, you've grown quite a lot.'

'I don't think so, Uncle.'

'No, not in height – you've broadened out more. Must be the good food you've had?'

'Not likely – the food is terrible, but I like the school. I don't know whether it likes me, though!'

'Of course it does. Come on, Paul, I've got a new car to show you.' Paul liked the new Mercedes.

'What sort of speed can you do in this, Uncle? I see the speedo tops 150 kilometres.'

'I don't do that sort of speed, Paul, though no doubt it would do that.' They continued the small talk, but there was already a strained relationship between them. Heide was longing to ask the boy all sorts of questions about St Peter's, but he didn't.

'How's Hilda?' asked the boy.

'Not too well, Paul – she's growing old now – in fact, I've managed to get her widowed sister to move in and help. You'll like her – she's called Martha.'

'I'm sorry to hear that, Uncle. Is Hilda ill in bed?'

'No, she is able to get up and about, but she gets unpleasant headaches – I didn't tell you about it as I didn't want to worry you.'

When Paul met Hilda he was shocked to see how much she had aged. She embraced him warmly.

The next day, his first at home for the Easter holidays, he reported to the Youth Movement Headquarters in Hamburg. He had asked Heide at breakfast if he would take him into Hamburg. He said he had written to some Hamburg school friends arranging to meet them for the day, and he would be home about six in the evening.

'Are you going to the Youth Movement place?' Heide had asked him in the car.

'Yes, Uncle. That's all right, isn't it?'

'Yes and no, Paul. I had hoped that perhaps you would have changed your mind about them – you said nothing about it in your letters home, nor when we were talking last night.'

'Well, you know what it is, Uncle, I have so many friends there and I just want to see them again – particularly to tell them about England.'

Heide had reluctantly dropped Paul in the centre of Hamburg and within a few minutes the boy was entering the Movement's offices. How wonderful he felt again! From the first Heil Hitler to his meeting with Seebohm in the afternoon, he felt he was truly at home once more.

Paul gave a lengthy description of St Peter's. Seebohm could detect no change in the boy's loyalty to the Party – he questioned him closely and was satisfied that the boy had managed to completely disguise his devotion to the Party. Paul had crossed the first hurdle, and Seebohm knew that great benefits could be obtained in the future. He relished the impact his report about the boy would have in Berlin.

His one great fear had been any influence the school's religious teaching might have had on Paul, but Paul reassured him. 'Herr Seebohm, you ask me about the Christian teaching. This is very powerfully stressed at the school. There are many services in the school chapel, as the church is called, one every day and two on Sundays. I think that if Christ did exist then he would have approved of our Party. Just as we are destined to greatness as a nation, so was He. The Bible tells us that He came into the world to right its wrongs – and that is what our Führer is going to do. It must be right to hate the Jews, for look what they did to Him!'

Seebohm, a graduate of Gottingen University, was convinced of the boy's cooperation in his plan, and congratulated himself on his assessment and judgement of Paul.

'I did find,' continued Paul, 'that there were some occasions when I badly wanted to speak and talk about our Party – but somehow or other I managed to overcome the temptation and obey your instructions that on no account was I to do this.'

'It is all wonderful – you are young, Paul, but not so far from manhood. A great future awaits you – you will one day be in a unique position to help your Führer and your country, of this I am certain. During your holidays I want you to attend the Movement's meeting at least twice a week, but you must somehow avoid upsetting your uncle Heide. Since I saw him and heard your later report of his disloyalty to our Party, his position has become confused. There is no doubt that he is totally against us, but it is necessary for him to know nothing of our plan for you. He has recently been engaged in trying to arouse hatred against us with many of his German friends. These people are carefully watched and at the right moment some sort of action will be taken. your uncle may even go to live in England, but in view of the need for you to come home each holiday to Germany, this must be prevented. Not by force if possible, so Paul, you must somehow put his mind at rest in regard to you.

'You mean, Herr Seebohm, I should pretend that I have lost interest in the Party?'

'Yes, I think that would be best, so that he at any rate does not suddenly decide to leave. Continue to report his anti-Party ideas to us, but neither agree nor disagree with him.'

'I understand, Herr Seebohm.'

'Heil Hitler.'

They then went their separate ways.

Paul's second term at St Peter's – the summer one in 1935 – was notable for three important developments: his good work in the classroom enabled the boy to reach a sufficient standard to gain promotion for the new school year to the class studying for matriculation; his belief in the Nazi Party was severely tested; and his homosexuality was stopped dead in its tracks by the astute action of the headmaster.

Just before half term, the School Debating Society had chosen for its motion 'That this house is convinced of the sincerity of the Nazi Party at present engaged in the modernisation and development of Germany'.

Paul and his friend John attended the debate, which was defeated by a large majority. But during the session, one sixth-former had aroused great sympathy in his attack upon the brutal methods the Nazis were using to gain domination throughout the country. The speaker's argument was almost an exact crib of an article which had appeared in a national newspaper, but it was so well delivered that the house had been held spellbound, shocked by some of the facts that were produced. Most of England was still apathetic about Hitler and indifferent to his policies – these boys were merely repeating views held not only by some of their fathers but also by the nation's press.

As the debate finished, John turned to Paul. 'Are those things really going on against people who disagree with Hitler?'

'I believe so, but the history of England is not exactly free from blemishes in the treatment of its opposers and enemies,' Paul replied defiantly.

'Maybe, Paul, but Jews aren't quite ignorant natives. Why doesn't your country like them?'

The opportunity to state the Nazis' case, and perhaps thereby reveal his complete devotion to the Nazis, was prevented by the call-over bell. The matter was forgotten for some days but John returned to it one evening in the dormitory.

'My father says that one day we'll be at war with Germany again – if that does happen, we will give you a darn good hiding, Paul,' he laughed.

'Don't talk nonsense, John – as if that could happen! I wouldn't swap Germany for this place.'

'You know, Paul, I certainly wouldn't fight for your country. What horrible things the Germans are doing to people – no, definitely, I'd rather have a beating from old Motts than lift a finger to help your crowd.'

'Is that so? Well, let me tell you that we would knock the blazes out of you if we had to. In fact—' He had to stop, for the shout of 'Lights out' by a house prefect also meant no more talking.

The two boys slept next to each other. Later that night Paul crept into John's bed. Mr Motts rarely went into the dormitories after lights out. If he did, for a reason best known to himself, he gave ample warning of his approach by coughing and shuffling his feet outside the door.

On this occasion the warning went unheeded, for Paul had fallen asleep in John's bed. Motts quietly walked the length of the dormitory – and saw one bed unoccupied and two heads on the pillow of the next bed.

Roberts, the House Captain, had heard the house master enter the dormitory, and had seen him walk to the far end. He sat up in his bed as Motts returned.

'Anything wrong, sir?' Roberts asked quietly.

'Come along to my room immediately.'

Roberts put on his dressing gown. Motts's door was open, but he knocked and waited to be summoned in.

'Come in, Roberts, and shut the door,' Motts said. 'You are unaware of what I have just seen. I hope you will be surprised to hear that in your dormitory, at this very moment, two boys are in bed together. I am not sure who they are, but you will return now, wake them up without disturbing any other boys, and bring them along here immediately.'

'Yes, sir, I – I certainly did not know.'

On his return to the dormitory, Roberts touched Paul on the shoulder. 'Wake up,' he whispered, 'wake up.'

Outside, in the changing room, Roberts said, 'What the hell do you think you are doing?'

Paul said nothing.

'Wait here, Heide.'

Roberts returned with Bright. 'Heide apparently does not want to say anything, so I won't ask you either. Now both of you go and get your dressing gowns and don't wake anyone up.'

It was Roberts' last term – he had won a scholarship to Oxford. His disgust at finding the boys in bed together was topped by the shame it brought to his house and by the fact that Motts had caught him in his failure as a house captain – and Roberts was furious.

'You two bloody fools,' he said. 'About five minutes ago Mr Motts came in to the dormitory. You've been caught by him. I only wish I had made the discovery and I would then have had the joy of tanning the life out of both of you. I'm to take you both to him immediately.'

Roberts went into Motts' room first. 'They're outside now, sir. It's Heide and Bright. I'm sorry, sir, shall I send them in together or separately?'

'Thank you, Roberts. Send them both in.' Roberts told them to go in and he returned to the dormitory.

'Stand over there,' Motts said to the boys, pointing to the

fire place. He sat behind his desk. 'There is no need for me to enquire as to why you were in Bright's bed, Heide. You both are in your sixteenth year and therefore fully aware of the gravity of what has happened. I would like to ask you one question: how long has this been going on?'

'Since the early part of last term, sir,' replied Heide. He was showing no remorse or fear.

'It's just something that happened, sir,' said Bright.

'Have you been doing this with any other boys?'

They both shook their heads.

'Therefore I can hope, if you are telling the truth, that no one else has become infected by your association. I am not going to beat you now because the shame that you have brought on your house and, for that matter, on the school is too big a matter for me to handle. I shall report to the headmaster in the morning and he will be seeing you in the course of the day. If you have any decency left in you, I hope that this will be kept from the other boys. Go straight back to the dormitory and get into your own beds.'

On the way to the dormitory only Paul spoke.

'That, John, seems to be that.'

Chapter Twelve

The headmaster of St Peter's, William Raiment, had studied Greats in 1912, and from Oxford gained a lectureship to Yale, returning to England at the outbreak of war in 1914. He joined his regiment, the Oxford and Buckingham Light Infantry, served throughout the war with it, and by the armistice deserved the DSO that he was awarded. He was lucky to also get a Military Cross and eager to do all in his power to help create a happier and better world. He hated injustice and could not tolerate liars. He had dedicated himself to helping people in trouble, perhaps to justify the deaths of so many of his young friends in the war. It was therefore easy for him to choose his career – the education of boys. By 1928 he had become a house master at Rugby, and from over 500 applicants was chosen for the headmastership of St Peter's in 1932 at the age of 42.

He was the first lay headmaster to be appointed, for as this was a church school, the board had always preferred a clergyman. But his record, personality and character pushed him ahead of the other contenders. He was a very rare man – a brilliant scholar, a fine leader and an honest man. Had he entered politics he might have become an even rarer prime minister. He had the gift of being able to understand boys' problems and, although a believer in the cane, he tried with considerable success to impress upon his boys that the main lesson to learn in life as early as possible was that mistakes were made to be learned from.

His great understanding of human frailties and his sympathetic yet firm approach to human sins and errors, with the emphasis on learning from those failing, established trust and devotion from masters and prefects.

From his childless marriage, he acquired the absolute love of his wife, who had dedicated herself to helping her husband, giving him an even broader and more compassionate outlook.

Facially he resembled the Prince of Wales, having the same genuine smile. He ambled more than walked, and looked the part of a strong man ready to defend the cause of someone weaker. Such was the man whom Paul and John were fortunate to face after late call-over, the day after Motts' report. The Head had waited a day before acting.

'I am seeing you both together; now sit down,' he had said to the boys in his study. 'Have either of you said anything about this affair to other boys?'

'No, sir,' they both said together.

'You have both had a worrying thirty-six hours, then, and perhaps your penance has already started.'

He filled and lit his pipe. 'This is not the first time I've had to deal with this problem, but it is the first time that the evidence has been so certain. It is sometimes only a suspicion I have to work on, and the question of getting at the truth is so much more difficult. I generally find that the sense of shame will often make a boy deny any accusations made to him. You must both realise the seriousness of what has occurred, if only because if this kind of thing developed on a large scale it could ruin the name of a school, and I have known this to happen. I saw it break first-rate officers in the Army. When that happens, the tragic consequences to a man's career are sometimes out of all proportion to the sin of the deed itself. Are you both following me very closely?'

They had both got very dry lips and knees like putty, and felt that their stomachs were full of butterflies. Both were sitting on the forward edge of their chairs, and for the first time in their lives they were very frightened. They were indeed following very closely.

'You must of course realise that I can expel you immediately...' Paul's heart in particular missed many beats. 'I could send you out of here, your trunks can be packed by tomorrow midday and you could leave with them. Can you, Heide, suggest any reason why I should not do that?'

Paul could think of many – but instead he said weakly, 'No, sir, I can't think of a good enough reason why you should not do that.'

'And you, Bright?'

'I don't relish meeting my father should that happen, sir,' he replied honestly.

Raiment continued, 'I want you both to realise that for one boy to have an attraction for another is not uncommon. It is, however, dangerous when a physical like develops and, whether you believe it or not, it is evil. It is a sin! If you have any belief in God at all, it follows that He could not approve of his children abusing a feeling that God, if you like, invented to ensure the continuance of the human race. If He had made it an unpleasant experience, then the race would not have got much further than the Garden of Eden, would it?'

The two boys just looked at him and made no reply. 'At the same time, He gave Man free will, whereby each individual can choose between right and wrong. If He had not done this, then the world would have been filled with morons – machines almost.' He paused. 'Your kind of unnatural friendship is often the result of boredom, but I don't think this applies to you two, for you both seem to be doing well. I take it that you like it here?'

'Oh yes, sir,' said Bright.

'Yes, sir,' replied Paul.

Raiment said nothing for what seemed an age. He just looked at them and they stared back.

'You must understand that what is dangerous about your act with one another is what it might lead to in later life.

THE TRIUMPH OF LOVE AND LIBERTY

Unless supreme efforts are made now to control your emotions, then the time might come when you would do these unnatural, objectionable things to persons much younger than yourselves and so poison further minds. Can you visualise for a moment that you are in charge of men – a serving officer, say? What hope would you have in gaining the respect of men in your control if you became involved in such a demoralising situation?'

Raiment was determined to try to prevent these two young lives from being wrecked at such an early stage.

'Bright, I want you to wait outside until you're called. Heide, you stay in here.'

When Paul was on his own, Raiment went on. 'Heide, who encouraged whom?'

'I did the encouraging, sir. Bright is not really in any way to blame. I'm sorry, sir.'

'How long have you been doing this sort of thing, Heide?'

'Oh, I suppose about two years, sir. A young man I met on a skiing holiday started it. I still see him when I'm home – at least I sometimes see him. He lives in Hanover.'

'Heide, you have got to stop your association with him – that's the first hurdle to overcome. I hope to be able to prove to you that it can be controlled. I am not going to expel either of you, but there will be certain rules that you will have to obey implicitly. I am not going to beat either of you, because that will not be the answer to your problem,' he went on.

'For the rest of this term and the next, for that matter, you will report to me once a week – we will discuss when later. You can continue being friendly with Bright, but I think you realise that should you be unable to exercise control of your feelings, then, for his sake alone, I may be forced to send you away from here. But I want you to understand that I do not think that you will fail either of us. Is that perfectly clear?'

'Yes. Yes, sir.'

'And lastly, two points. You can make yourself master of your feelings. When unpleasant thoughts enter your mind throw them out, and if you cannot do that, then for heaven's sake get on with a job of work and thereby occupy your mind with better and cleaner things. Don't think it can't be done, because it can, provided you have strength of character to do it. I believe you and Bright have this strength, so don't let me down and don't let yourself down. Second, as no one else knows about this, except Mr Motts and Mr Roberts, no one else need ever know, because I will be seeing those two about my decision. Now, out you go and send Bright in.'

Later, the two boys met in the dormitory. It was nearly lights out.

'I can make the effort – can you, John?' Paul said.

'I reckon so – it's worth it anyway. Do you know what the old man said to me? That if we didn't stop doing these things then if we marry then it might be difficult to have children. I don't know what on earth he's talking about, but as far as I'm concerned I'm cutting it out.'

'John,' replied Paul, 'I've made love to a girl. I assure you it's more pleasant. I'm with you all the way.'

Chapter Thirteen

Heide had many times wanted to quit Germany, but on each occasion he was delayed by circumstances. Hilda's health did not improve and she became a semi-invalid. She couldn't contemplate leaving her country, and Heide couldn't leave her. Then, although he knew he was being watched and having his mail censored by the Nazis, he had to admit no action had been taken against him. His business, too, prospered. In the middle of 1936 he had obtained the sole German agency for a leading English textile manufacturer. He began to feel that perhaps, after all, a more liberal form of Nazism would arise. He had also become concerned by the indifferent and obtuse attitude of the English members of the Anglo-German society. Their enthusiasm had quickly waned, maybe understandably after Hitler's support for Italy at the time of the invasion of Abyssinia. But this drop in support from the English side made the task of keeping the Germans interested very difficult.

Heide's health, too, had unexpectedly caused him concern – shooting pains across his back had been diagnosed as severe lumbago. The doctor reckoned this was a result of living in the trenches during the war.

During the Christmas term of 1936, he had visited St Peter's, met the headmaster and then taken Paul out for the day. That night on his return to London he had arranged to meet Colonel Bedford.

They met at Heide's hotel in Park Lane and over dinner the boy's future was discussed.

'How's Paul?' the colonel had asked.

'He's settled down so well. I'm very grateful to you, Colonel, for getting the boy into St Peter's.'

'If he can get into university, that will be a great step up for him,' remarked Bedford.

'He won't be doing that,' said Heide. 'When I saw Raiment this afternoon, he seemed certain that the boy should sit for Sandhurst. So there you are – he'll be following in your footsteps.'

'That's grand news. Why the Army, though?'

'He's very keen on the training corps at school and apparently thrives on the spit and polish – his school reports have always borne this out. I didn't mention this at all today, though—' Heide paused. 'He still attends the Hitler Youth Movement meetings during the holidays.'

'Good thing too – I hear that it keeps the boys and girls out of trouble. But I've also heard that your country is hell bent on rearmament. That sort of thing won't keep you out of trouble, though.'

Heide didn't reply. 'You know,' he said, 'it's remarkable how England manages to get the best wines – take this '29 Rhine wine – it's delicious and certainly the best.'

'If, Herr Heide, you stay at this hotel, you'll always get the best. Did you know that all the laundry is sent to Normandy for cleaning? After washing, they bleach the linen by laying it on the beaches. If they can afford to do that, they can certainly afford to get the best wines, don't you agree?' Bedford said.

'Indeed, that is something! England is certainly the best place in the world to live, if you have money. I haven't any money,' he joked.

'I don't believe that for one moment,' grinned Bedford. 'But I do believe that Germany is rearming at the moment.

'Please, Colonel,' Heide looked over his shoulder – the dining room was half empty, 'can we keep off the subject of what my country is doing and not doing?'

'I'm sorry, Herr Heide, I didn't mean anything in particular – just conversation, that's all.'

Should Heide say what had occurred? He pushed the potatoes of his sole bonne femme to the side of his plate.

'I may see something of you in Germany next year Herr Heide.' He heard Bedford's voice as if in the distance. *I like this man*, he thought. *I like this country. What's so different about England? I've always tried to live a decent life.* He tried to think of the regrets of his life – fewer, probably, than other Germans and British, French, Italian, European, American. But Britain had her empire – was that where the difference lay? And her empire made the have-nots envious. If Britain hadn't an empire then perhaps other nations would not want to expand overseas. Of course they would – nationalism breeds power, breeds greed, breeds Hitler. 'There is therefore every likelihood that I will go to the British Embassy in Berlin for a spell,' the colonel was saying.

The word 'Berlin' brought Heide back to his untouched bonne femme.

'You may like the wine, but you certainly don't go for the fish, Herr Heide?' Bedford said.

'I'm sorry, Colonel, you were saying that you might be going to Berlin – to work or play?'

'No, I was saying for work – I don't think that I would go there for play.'

'And why not? It can be quite a city, when it makes an effort.'

'That's the trouble – when it makes an effort. I like my play to be spontaneous.'

'When will you be there?'

'I should think by about the middle of next June.'

Heide had to tell him. No one could possibly overhear now. When he spoke he did so quietly and his eyes looked at Bedford's hands.

'Colonel, you remember two years ago when we first met?'

'Very well, Herr Heide – I seem to recall that we discussed ways of putting the world and Germany to right.'

'A short time after that I had a very late visit one night from the police – worse, the Gestapo, Hitler's secret police.' Heide's hand was trembling. He coughed, reached for his glass, and knocked it over with the outside of his hand. The wine flowed over the table in a thin stream towards Bedford. The two men watched it and didn't move. It found another course, reached the edge of the table and trickled over the side.

A waiter came across to the table.

'You know, Herr Heide,' said Bedford, 'good wine in a glass looks like perfection – but out of a glass or bottle it looks like any other liquid.'

The waiter had cleared the mess of wine.

Heide continued, 'They had obtained an accurate version of our conversation. I have been watched ever since, and the strain of it all is beginning to have its effect on me.'

'I imagine it must be,' said Bedford. He paused, 'Yes I know about that – you see, I told them.'

Chapter Fourteen

Heide just sat and looked at Bedford. He couldn't be in England – he must be suffering from hallucinations. There was a swishing of noise in his ears. He knew that he had stood up and that Bedford had too. It was the colonel who eased him back into his chair.

Bedford then returned to the opposite side of the table and stood facing Heide.

'If you would like to go to your room for a while, I'll take you there,' he said.

The German sat looking up at Bedford. The colonel was joking; that's what it was, he was joking.

'I feel better now, Colonel. Your English sense of humour is out of taste this time. Please don't make fun of such events that are happening every day and night in Germany.'

Bedford took out a cigarette, passed one to Heide, and lit them both before replying.

'I can assure you I was not joking. I have never been more serious in my life. Now, may I suggest that we both go to your room and continue the conversation there?'

Bedford got up first and Heide followed him.

Heide didn't recall going up in the lift, but he remembered getting out the room key, shutting the door behind Bedford and sitting on the edge of his bed.

Bedford spoke first. 'I am sorry, Herr Heide, deeply sorry to have confused you – that is the understatement of the year – to have shocked and distressed you. But it had to be done sometime on this visit of yours, and I thought that the right moment had arrived.'

'Colonel Bedford,' Heide said softly and with the same pitch and tone in his voice, 'you obviously meant what you said – and you are correct in speaking of my present state of mind as being shocked and confused.

The colonel cut in, 'Heide, let me start at the beginning, and I promise you that it will be short and to the point. I did report you through the German section. Before I leave this room tonight I have got to convince you of the truth of my little story. If I fail in that, it is possible that you will not return to Germany. There is too much at stake to contemplate failure in my mission. I work in counter-espionage – I am an agent to the Germans, but still fond enough of my king and country to work and die for England. How this happened is known only to the head of British Intelligence, and now you. For a period of six years from 1929 to 1935 I was given leave of absence. My assignment was to gain the complete confidence of the German authorities, convince them of my hatred of everyone and anything British. You can see how useful my knowledge of the German language has been. The situation today is that I have – or should I say, *hope* to have – the confidence of German espionage. Now, Herr Heide, have another cigarette and ask some questions.'

'I am a true German patriot, Colonel – because my country is ruled by the wrong people, this does not mean to say that it will always be so. Of what possible help can I be to an enemy of my country?' He refused the offered cigarette.

'I think, Herr Heide, of great help! You realise the risk I took tonight in telling you my story? Do you imagine that months of work and thought have not gone into that?' He continued speaking at a much quicker rate. 'I know that you abhor the Nazis, especially for what they are doing not only to Germans who disagree with their policies, but to other nationals whose religions they don't like or want. The speech you made some years ago at Brighton got wide publicity and it didn't miss our attention. We reckoned that speech was made by you on behalf of thousands of Germans who had had enough of dictators, who want to live in peace and who place the individual above the state. That's the trouble with any socialist party, either ours or your kind of national one, eventually the individual is sacrificed on the state altar.' He paused to let that sink in, and then continued speaking slowly, 'Of course, if there are no Germans who think like you, then I'm gravely mistaken and at the same time despair of there ever being a world at peace – but I know I'm not mistaken. There are thousands, hundreds of thousands of you who want peace. Your culture is as good as any in the world.' Bedford lit his cigarette and then said brutally, 'If that speech of yours was a pack of lies and if you've had a change of heart about Hitler, then I for one will welcome another war with your country, and when we've won that one, I shall pray for Germany to be broken up into as many tiny states as possible. I sometimes wish that had been done in 1918.'

Heide asked Bedford to light his cigarette. His hand was trembling with emotion.

'What can I do to help in the destruction of Hitler and the Nazis?' was all Heide said.

In June of the following year Bedford was working in the military section of the British Embassy in Berlin, and by July he had received the final briefing on Paul's future from his Nazi contacts. The boy was to stay at St Peter's until the end of the summer term of 1938 – if possible, the Sandhurst entry should be made for the college winter term of the same year.

Of all the information given to Heide by Bedford, both men agreed that no contact between the two men would ever be made in Germany.

Heide's apparent conversion to Nazism was rapid. During Paul's Christmas holidays in 1936, Heide attended many Nazi meetings with the boy and even did voluntary office work for the Youth Movement at the Hamburg centre. By the end of that holiday Paul was able to report to the Party that his uncle Heide had taken the decision to devote his energies in future to the good of the Party.

The Hamburg Gestapo were pleased by Heide's outward conversion, but were not convinced completely. At a Nazi rally held in the city in the summer of 1937, Heide had spoken in support of Nazism, his main theme being that he had learned the errors of his ways and now saw how much good the Führer was achieving for the Fatherland. He said that any doubts he had nursed were completely dispelled by the example the leader had given to the youth of the country, and how impressed he had been with the progress made in establishing a sound economy. The road-building alone had modernised the German communications overnight.

The subsequent gain to British Intelligence was not great. The information he carried to London on his business journeys was of minor importance – some aerial photos he had obtained of Hamburg were of limited use, for the dock area was excluded. Information he obtained for the Admiralty about U-boat pens at Bremerhaven was already known. But he had been relieved of much mental anguish since he began working for British espionage, and he did not even consider that he was a traitor to his own country. He regarded Hitler as an evil moment in German history. Any efforts that could be directed towards his downfall were completely justified. Few Germans were able to do anything positive. To show outward dislike for Nazism resulted every time in the concentration camp. One either became someone like Pastor Niemöller – the anti-Nazi theologian – or a passive resister, but the latter had no chance of success. Heide knew of such men who openly flouted the Nazis, but these people were continually in fear of political prison and death. He had heard of a lawyer, Konrad Adenauer, who openly showed little respect for the Party, but such small pebbles were lost on the vast beach of Nazism.

The apathy and indifference of the world beyond Germany gave no hope or encouragement to the German opposers of Hitler – the near-comic behaviour of the League of Nations merely intensified the hopelessness of Germans who might wish to oppose the regime. How easy it was for the British to say to Heide in London, 'You all put Hitler there!' He could equally argue, and often did, that the Allies created the situation for the man's rise to power in the first place, by the inconsistencies of the treaty following the Great War.

But for Heide, the greatest worry was Paul. The boy seemed to have settled down so well at St Peter's but in the holidays he became lost and submerged by the glamour of the Youth Movement. It was imperative that Heide stay on in Germany, where he was now forced to watch and outwardly agree with the boy's support for the Nazis.

Towards the end of 1937 Heide met Bedford in London. They had arranged a later meeting at the Hotel Metropole in Brighton, where Heide was staying for the weekend in order to see Paul.

Bedford had downplayed the man's fears.

'The boy's having a very good English education, and I don't think your fears are really justified – the effect of the Christian teaching is bound to make itself felt one day. In any case, he's a British National, and it won't be long now before he'll be a serving officer in the British Army – in just a few years, Herr Heide.'

'But supposing there is a war? What on earth will his position be then, Colonel Bedford? Can't you see the dangerous position that is developing for the boy's future?' He waited for a moment or so and then continued, 'I am not worried about myself for in the event of war I will of course stay in Germany, but—'

'Herr Heide,' Bedford interrupted, 'one of the reasons I am

seeing you is to discuss your future position. In the event of war we will require you to come and live in England.'

'That's nonsense, Colonel! Of what possible help can I be in this country? In any case, I don't think there will be a war, for at the rate he's going, Hitler will get what he wants without one. I may add, Colonel, that when I agreed to work for your country it was based on the supposition that there would not be a war, for I hope that freedom of speech and all the other freedoms will return to my country without hostilities. I hope that the world will awaken in time to put pressure on Hitler and perhaps by economic sanctions bring about an economic collapse of Germany. We can then re-elect the type of government that my people deserve.'

'Herr Heide,' Bedford exclaimed, 'what sense does that make? Your work for us is based on the possibility of another war with Germany. You are with us for the long-term objective of defeating the Reich in war. Should that happen, then any contribution you have made to the fall of the Nazis – and I particularly omit the word *German* – any contribution you have made will have been the right one because then will be the moment for the German people to get another chance to create a peaceful society.'

'If we have another war, neither the world nor Germany would have a chance to create anything – another war will be Armageddon.'

'All the information we have asked from you has been military. There is only one hope of preventing a war and that is for us to be so strong that Hitler won't dare to start one for fear of losing.'

'This is in the future, Colonel. For the present, why should I have to come to England should a war start?'

'Because, Herr Heide, it wouldn't be fair to leave you in your country. Your age, for one—' He paused and then continued, 'Although in law you are a traitor to your country, in fact you might be able at some time to exert an influence on world opinion and help create an impression of trust. You're not betraying Germany, you're betraying Nazism, the National Socialists. If you are not caught, then no one need ever know of your secret work for England. That's another good reason for you to leave at the appropriate time.'

'And Paul,' said Heide, 'what of him? Do you think it will be all cut and dried for him? Suppose in the final analysis he doesn't want to join the British Army? For the life of me, I cannot understand or believe that he will do this. You haven't seen him during the holidays and had the experience of witnessing his fervour for Hitler and his ways!'

'I think it best for you to cross that hurdle when and if you ever come to it,' Bedford lied. His own plans were already made for the boy's future. 'You're seeing Paul tomorrow?'

'Yes, as you know I'm remaining for the next week to attend the school's end-of-term carol service and then take the boy back with me to Hamburg.'

'That's excellent, Herr Heide, and it gives you the perfect excuse to remain in this country for a few more days.' Bedford continued, 'Do you still refuse to accept any payment for the work you are doing for us?'

'Certainly, Colonel – if I ever have to do that then I would feel a traitor. I am a very rich man, as you no doubt realise. I have also been having my fees from my English agencies paid into a bank in London. It's quite a considerable amount.'

'As you wish, Herr Heide. You find that the message codes we send are efficient and foolproof?'

'Yes to that too – I've never received the emergency one. I am told it will be in the form of a telegram worded "Your agency in London requires your immediate presence here to discuss the new contract" – is that correct?'

'I don't concern myself with the details – if that's what you've been told by London then it would be so. We will probably meet in town within the next few months. You mustn't worry about Paul, you know. I'd wager that the education he's getting will hold out against the Nazi doctrine. I'm sure you can be certain of that.'

Bedford then left, but Heide continued to feel uneasy about the boy. He determined to speak to the headmaster, Raiment, while he was visiting the school. As he tried to sleep he pondered over Paul's future. The salient point in the British character was the belief the British had in themselves. Outwardly they often seemed unsure, but inwardly they were so very sure. Paul had shown outward confidence. Heide wondered if St Peter's had given the boy any inner calm.

Chapter Fifteen

William Raiment was waiting to see Heide, even though the appointment had been made at short notice and came at the end of term – usually a busy period.

'Herr Heide, I am delighted to have the opportunity to have a chat with you about Paul,' Raiment opened the conversation. 'His house master, Mr Motts, is particularly pleased with your boy's progress this term. There is every chance of his becoming captain of his house next term.'

'That makes me feel very proud of him, Headmaster. You know at one time I gave serious thought to sending him to Salem, in Germany – but for Colonel Bedford's quick action on my behalf, this would have happened. I think that my country is against developing individuality – it's swimming against the current of world opinion.'

Raiment smiled and said, 'You know in many ways our system here tends to create the herd instinct but of course in the boys' last years to my mind the most important positions of responsibility bring out the best – and on occasion – the worst in them. Paul has developed into a young man of promise; his first few terms were difficult – you no doubt read between the lines in his reports. I see no reason why an Army career should not be ideal for him. He has the luck to have an amount of rebelliousness in him and yet he appreciates the need for discipline.'

'Headmaster, does he ever talk about the present system of government in Germany?'

'No, not to my knowledge. He does have a reputation for talking of Germany's mountains and scenery though. He often derides the heights of our South Downs in comparison with your beautiful ranges. My own view of Germany is one of concern. Do you support the Third Reich, Herr Heide?'

Heide wanted to ask the questions, so he wasn't prepared for this. After a bad start, he recovered.

'Naturally there are many difficulties. I was in the Army in the last war and—'

The headmaster politely asked where Heide had been, and the two men quickly realised that they had not been on the same fronts. Heide continued, 'From that war we have not recovered.' He stalled, waiting for Raiment to talk; he didn't. 'The history of modern Germany is so disconnected. Nothing seems continuous except for the apparent ease with which dictators become established. I cannot say that I approve of most of the present methods used by Herr Hitler to stay in power.' He stopped, hoping that would be sufficient; it was.

'Why, Herr Heide, do you ask about your boy's interest or otherwise in Germany?'

'During the holidays he attends all the Youth Movement activities in Hamburg – much of the dogma is bad, and I worry about the effect it might have on his development.'

'Everything now is relative, Herr Heide,' answered Raiment. 'We try here to develop a dependence on God. In most cases we succeed – at any rate, judging by the records of public service of many of our Old Boys. We also, I think, have a certain amount of success in creating self-confidence, and we try to instil in the boys the importance of having belief in themselves. Paul has outwardly gone on the right lines, after a shaky start. We can only hope that the qualities taught here have given him the foundation to build his future life on. But who can really tell how any human mind will, in the end, develop?'

'Headmaster, as far as I'm concerned you have answered my questions, and many thanks for not only giving me your time but also for being so honest. I often consider how good it would be for the relationship between our two countries if an exchange between the students could be made – if we were to send some of our boys to you, and vice versa.'

'I agree, Herr Heide. May I say now that I hope your country moves into better times. I happen to know that there are some very good Germans, with a capital G. There are many people of goodness and wisdom, even if at the moment they are obscured by evil and apparent stupidity. We also have our share of them over here!'

After the meeting with the headmaster Heide saw Mr Motts for a short chat. There was little the two had to say to each other. Motts, hating the Germans and everything German, was uneasy in Heide's presence. Heide, sensing Motts' feelings, left as soon as he could.

In the Easter holidays of 1938 Heide decided to break the length of time Paul spent with the Youth Movement in Hamburg and arranged for the boy to go on a skiing holiday in Arosa, Switzerland. Paul had grown into a handsome young man. He had the habit of walking with a swagger and held himself very upright, making him look even taller than his six feet. He was a fine athlete, and excelled in rugby and swimming.

Paul was sure that the future of Germany rested upon the youth of the country. His early friendship with John Bright had not flourished. It declined rapidly after the meeting with the headmaster over the two boys' relationship with each other. He had never ceased to thank the head for that talk. He realised now that had he been expelled, it could have meant the ruination of any plans Seebohm and the Nazis had for him. He had a habit of lying awake after lights out at school, and his mind was then occupied with thoughts of Germany, and in particular with the Nazis. He had at an early stage at St Peter's built a shield around any criticism of the Führer. To him, Hitler was God. How thankful he had been for the enlightenment he had gained at an early age. From the start of his time at St Peter's, Christianity had meant nothing to him. Many of the boys disliked the compulsory twice-daily chapel services, so he was quickly encouraged in his own dislike. He treated his confirmation service as a joke and, along with many others, gained consolation for the compulsory attendance at Holy Communion by having a swig of wine at the altar.

His natural aptitude as a leader earned him a certain kind of popularity. No one individual could call himself a close friend of Paul. Not even John Bright. He had always enjoyed his work in the Officers' Training Corps, but now that his name was entered for Sandhurst he had become impatient to know just when Seebohm would say, 'And now you can come to Germany.' When he had mentioned this to the man on his last holiday. Seebohm had told him not to be impatient. He might not end up going to Sandhurst anyway, but he was to continue on the assumption that this would happen. Seebohm had noticed the boy's muddled expression and had then played the problem down.

When Paul told Seebohm of the skiing holiday his uncle had arranged, the latter had agreed to it. It was only for a fortnight and Paul would have a further week in Hamburg before returning to England. Seebohm also suggested that tactful support by Paul for the Nazis while he was in Switzerland might also sow some small but useful seeds for the Party there.

Paul's ready acceptance of the holiday pleased Heide. He was grateful to have the boy out of Hamburg, not only because of the Youth Movement, but also because of his own situation. Since Hilda's death the previous November her sister Martha had only just managed to cope with the housekeeping. She grumbled all of the time. He intended to let her go after Paul's return to school. He had been assured the services of a middle-aged widow whose docker husband had been killed in a crane accident at the dockside.

Paul's lone train journey to Switzerland was full of interest for him. The trip across the depth of Germany to Basle brought home to him as could nothing else the industrial strength of the country. Enormous factories with their chimneys belching smoke, the roads with heavy traffic, both civil and military, and the towns and cities bustling, efficient. And Nazi banners – they seemed to be flying from every building.

At Basle he changed trains and boarded one which had come from Calais. He would stay on this train until Chur and then change once more, taking the mountain railway up to Arosa. He entered a compartment occupied by a married couple and their daughter.

'Do you mind if I sit in here?' he had asked in German.

'Of course not,' the father had replied in English, in the way the English abroad take for granted that their language will be understood.

Paul looked at the girl – Paula Stevens, as he was later to discover. He thought how pretty she looked, her fair hair shining under a white woollen cap. When she smiled she had beautiful white teeth and merry blue eyes. The Stevens were going to Arosa and were staying at the same hotel as Paul. Neither Paula nor Paul could foresee how deep rooted their attachment would become.

Chapter Sixteen

The Stevens lived in London. The father, George, a senior civil servant in Whitehall, was a quiet efficient-looking man. His wife Margaret was tall, thin and snobby faced. Paul was encouraged by her in his friendship with Paula. 'My dear,' she had said to her husband, 'he goes to St Peter's.' Her husband did not like the boy but continued his normal habit of agreeing with his wife. 'Yes,' he said, 'he seems a nice lad.' He wanted to say that he couldn't stand the boy's superior ingratiating manner – obviously too much of the German in him.

Paul and Paula were drawn to each other from the first moment of meeting. The likeness of their names made them laugh, and they both felt their mutual attraction.

For the non-skiers, the centre of life in the village was the frozen lake where the skaters performed to the quiet recorded music. Paula left the hotel on the first morning before Paul. He passed the lake carrying his skis and saw her doing a skater's waltz on the ice. He could not skate well but he watched her. She was looking lovely in her white sweater and short pleated skirt. He thought he had never seen anything more graceful. She skimmed over the ice like a bird and he decided he must learn at once. She was a good teacher but he knew he could never skate as well as Paula. He suggested skiing, but she had never been taught.

'I'll soon teach you,' said Paul.

'I haven't any skis.'

'I hadn't any skates an hour ago – come on, I'll get you some skis!' He went on, 'You must learn, it's great fun! Then we can go off for long expeditions to the mountains, just the two of us.'

He showed her the different moves and turns on the lower slopes. She tried to copy him amid a great deal of laughing and tumbling in the snow. She had her first ski downhill and arrived alarmed and in a heap at the bottom.

'I feel I can't stop!'

'That'll come,' laughed Paul and by the end of the first week she could do snowplough turns with the best of them.

Paul then took her on some long runs. There were very few ski lifts, so this meant much climbing. Skins were put on the skis, and it often took most of the morning to get to the top of the mountains. There were numerous variations of runs down, the village being surrounded by mountains; the highest, the Weisshorn, took the whole morning to climb. The afternoon could be spent in a leisurely descent, stopping on the way down at three or four of the huts for refreshments and to sunbathe. It was on the last day but one that Paul took Paula on this run. It was Sunday, and a clear blue sky gave a setting of perfection. As the two slowly climbed they could hear the bells ringing for Mass in all the little churches for miles around; the clear mountain air was full of their chimes. Paul silently led the way. The spring snow was pure, the only sound that of the bells. He felt at peace and thought he was totally in love with Paula. He hadn't wanted to make the kind of love with her that he had been shown by Anna Stucklen. He had kissed her the previous evening in the little corner of the cellar bar at the hotel. Mrs Stevens had let them both go there alone. It was Paula's first kiss. The second occurred a while later when they had gone for a walk in the village. Paul walked her slowly back to the hotel with his arm around her shoulders. He hadn't wanted to fondle her in any other way.

They reached the top of the Weisshorn in the early afternoon. Outside the hut there were a dozen or so people.

In the distance they could see the peaks of the French and Italian Alps. Paula felt the mountains were like heaven; she felt nearer to God than she had ever felt before.

'Do you believe there is a God?' she suddenly said to Paul.

Paul looked at her – to him at that moment the only being that existed was her.

'I don't know, Paula.'

'That's a funny answer. I know there is because no man could ever create such beauty as we can see now.'

Paul turned his eyes away from her and, looking at the distant mountains, said, 'I would think that if a man was worried or distressed about anything, then he should come up here into this pure air, and alone with the sky, all his troubles would take on their right proportions and he would find peace.'

'In other words, Paul, his spirit would find peace, so he would know there was a God.' She looked at him.

'Come on, Paula, we're going down now,' was all he said, but then he continued, 'I will go down a short distance at a time and then when I stop, you take the exact course I have taken, and don't forget when you want to slow down, put your skis out in front of you in the shape of a V with your weight on the inside edges and when you want to turn, do the same thing and bring your weight onto the left ski to turn right and onto the right ski to turn left, and don't try to go too fast.'

They made a slow but safe descent which took most of the afternoon. They had stopped on the final run that would bring them to the hotel terrace. They could see Paula's parents. They waved and the Stevens waved back. Paul said suddenly, 'Paula, I love you very much. I know that I will never love anyone as much ever in my life.'

'Paul, I feel the same about you.' She was standing just below him. He leaned on his ski stick, lowering his head to kiss her lips. Her skis were pointing at a slight angle to the slope and she slowly slid backwards as he kissed her. She went back a few yards and then fell laughing into the snow, and when Paul skied to her side to help her up they finished the embrace. The snow on her lips made them both laugh. Mrs Stevens saw all this with a mixture of approval and dislike.

On his last night at Arosa, Paul asked Mrs Stevens if he would be allowed to keep in touch with her daughter.

'Of course, Paul, although you must both remember you're still very young – is that not so, dear?' she said to her husband. As she had asked him the previous day to say something to Paul about the kissing they had seen and to tell them that they were far too young to be doing that sort of thing, he was astonished at her open approval of the friendship. Here she had the chance to say something; but no, the responsibility was his, so he said, 'Yes, if you say so, but as Paul spends his holidays in Germany, there won't be much time to meet, will there?' He sat back in his chair rather pleased with himself.

'Oh, but George, perhaps we can arrange for Paul to spend some of his holiday with us?'

The inconsistency of women! He frowned, looked away, coughed and went on reading the three-day-old *Times*.

'That would be marvellous, Mrs Stevens. Thank you very much – I'd love to do that,' Paul said.

Back in Germany, Heide said, 'You look very fit and well, Paul. There's no need to ask you if you had a good time at Arosa.'

'It was terrific, Uncle, thank you,' and then Paul told him about Paula.

'She sounds a very nice girl, Paul, and I'm doubly pleased that she's English. There are some letters for you – I've put them in your room.'

One was from Fritz, now an air force officer and stationed outside Berlin. He hoped Paul was in good health and that when his schooling finished in England they would see each other. Paul tore this up. The other announced a Youth Movement meeting at which Herr Josef Goebbels, the Minister of Propaganda, was to speak. The rally, the biggest of its kind in Hamburg, was being held in the Public gardens the next day.

Paul appeared at breakfast the next morning in his Youth Movement uniform and wore the prominent Nazi armband on his sleeve. Heide assumed the boy was going to the Nazi meeting. He wanted to say so much, but remained silent.

Chapter Seventeen

On the day in June in 1938 when Colonel Bedford was arrested in his Berlin apartments by the Gestapo on a charge of plotting against the Third Reich, Herr Heide received in his Hamburg office a telegram from London: 'Your agency in London requires your immediate presence here to discuss the new contract.' He sat staring at the message for some minutes – he tried to fight back tears in his eyes but couldn't. He knew this meant the end of his living in Germany and for a time sat still, tears pouring down his face, full of regrets for his deceit against Germany. He suddenly hated Bedford, and the realisation of the miserable years that lay ahead for him in isolation in England made him want to phone the colonel in Berlin and then make a full confession to the German police. He asked his secretary to get the British embassy in Berlin on the line, then walked slowly to the office window. Neither he nor the world knew of Bedford's arrest until the following day.

Heide looked down at the wide Hamburg street below, busy with the midday traffic. For a moment he thought how easy it would be to jump out of the window. Then he saw and heard the band. Behind it were masses of uniformed Germans holding banners with swastikas, banners with anti-Jewish slogans. He saw a group suddenly break away from the main stream of the procession and hurl bricks through the shop windows opposite his office block. He saw them daub paint over the door, and a moment later the Jewish proprietor was dragged into the street. The poor wretch was clubbed to the ground and stripped of all his clothes. A hundred yards down the street he saw the group of police, who were merely standing and watching.

Then, as he stared at his own countrymen's conduct, he thought of Paul in England. His tears had now stopped. He walked away from the window and the phone rang. 'The British embassy on the phone for you, Herr Heide,' said his secretary.

'I'm sorry,' he said, and then, 'please cancel the call.'

There was a ship leaving Hamburg that night for Tilbury and he had no difficulty in arranging a booking. He left his office, taking all the necessary papers with him. A year or so previously he had rented an office near High Holborn in London, and that office had got duplicates of all his relevant business correspondence. He explained to his new housekeeper, 'I may be away in London for longer than usual. Take good care of everything.'

He wrote the following letter: 'To whom it may concern, this is to certify that Marlene Herwath has my, the owner's, full permission to remain in the house for as long as she wishes.' He sealed it in an envelope, saying it had instructions for her regarding the forwarding of post and that she was to open it if any post arrived for him. All the furniture and his lifelong belongings would be left behind. He told Marlene to have the rest of the day off, and spent the next hour packing a large suitcase, cramming as many clothes as he could into it. His boat was due to leave Hamburg at 10.00 p.m. and until seven he wandered aimlessly round the house, recalling the memories of a lifetime – the night his son had been born, the sad and sudden blow of his wife's death, the sombre funeral which followed, his days at home from the front, the day he brought young Paul home and the happiness he had seen on Hilda's face.

The taxi arrived just after seven. From then until his safe arrival in London the next evening, he travelled as though in a dream.

On the same evening the news broke on a shocked London of Colonel Bedford's arrest by the Nazis. Heide had missed the evening papers and went straight to bed on arrival at the hotel.

He saw the news in the next morning's newspapers. The banner headlines stared out at him 'Regular army officer arrested by Hitler', 'Seized in his rooms at Charlottenburg Strasse – our ambassador protests'. Heide's bedside phone rang.

'There is a Mr Edwards from your London agency to see you, sir,' said the receptionist.

'Thank you. Ask him to come up.'

Heide spoke first, showing the contact man the headlines about Bedford. 'Did you know about this when the message was sent to me?'

'We knew that Bedford had become very concerned about various Nazis he had recently met. He was being shadowed, he had sensed things were wrong. He was leaving Berlin today. We were too late.'

'He will, of course, be sent back to this country by the Nazis,' said Heide.

'No,' said Edwards. 'There is nothing that we can do for him. The government will no doubt make loud noises but there is no hope of active support for him. Our government will merely deny the charges. What the Nazis decide to do is anyone's guess – there is a faint hope that Hitler may send him back to show the world how kind he is and how peaceful his intentions are.'

'It's terrible,' murmured Heide.

'And for you, Herr Heide, the instructions are that you do nothing. We are certain that Bedford will betray no one. Can you manage for money?'

'Yes, I have plenty in the bank over here—' He paused. 'Only my housekeeper in Hamburg knows that I am in London. I hope that I can return fairly soon.'

'Why, Herr Heide?'

'Oh, just to get back, that's all.' He knew this was impossible.

'That cannot happen. It would only be a matter of time before they caught up with you. No, Herr Heide, you are now in this country indefinitely. It is doubtful if you could ever return while the Nazis control Germany. I have been asked to tell you that when the Bedford crisis has calmed down, you should quietly ask for political asylum....' Edwards' conversation trailed off.

'I understand,' said Heide.

Later that day he phoned Raiment at St Peter's. 'I will be living in this country for a while,' he explained to the headmaster, 'but would you please not tell the boy this? I will write to him from here tonight.'

'Yes, of course, Herr Heide,' said Raiment. 'We all here are very worried about Colonel Bedford. Do you think there is any truth in the accusations made against him?'

'I don't know what to think. I'm very tired, Headmaster, and I must drop a line to Paul this evening. I hope we meet soon.'

'Of course, I realise – I look forward to seeing you here for Speech Day.'

'Thank you, Headmaster. I just cannot leave London at the moment. I hope you understand.'

Dear Paul,

For some time now I have been contemplating making a home in England. I am at the moment staying at this hotel and until further notice you should write to me here. I know how much you like Germany and of course there is no reason why we should not be there again one day. Since Hilda's death the house has seemed very lonely and I have so much business in this country that I thought I might just as well live over here for a while. I feel certain that Mrs Herwarth will look after the house.

THE TRIUMPH OF LOVE AND LIBERTY

I'm sorry I cannot get down for Speech Day. I know you will understand.
Your affectionate Uncle,
PS I expect there is much excitement about Colonel Bedford at St Peter's.

Paul received the letter with dismay, replied to it, and immediately reported its contents in a letter to Seebohm in Hamburg. The day Seebohm received Paul's letter, Heide's house in Hamburg was raided by the police. Herwath was evicted – she couldn't understand why. The letter left by Herr Heide was ignored by the police; as there had been mail to forward she had opened it that morning, as instructed by Heide. She was merely told to pack her bags and get out. The house was then searched and by the afternoon both it and its contents were commandeered on behalf of the glorious Reich.

On hearing the news from Hamburg, Heide was at a complete loss to understand how the Nazis had acted so quickly. Perhaps Colonel Bedford had given them the information. Whatever the reason, he realised that England would now be his home. He felt an inner determination to do all in his power to fight for the expulsion of Hitler from Germany. He hoped that he would himself return one day, helping to build a democratic society in his homeland.

The infamous and unjust trial of Bedford is now just another page in the history of Nazi oppression and tyranny. Not only were the proceedings held in secret, at no time were any British representatives allowed to see the man. The day before the end of Paul's last term at St Peter's the German court announced a verdict of guilty and a sentence of 25 years' imprisonment. Bedford was never heard of again – some believe he was shot shortly after the trial, others that he died in a concentration camp.

Shortly after the trial, Hitler suddenly demanded that the Sudeten districts of Czechoslovakia be ceded to Germany. Bedford was forgotten in the world's news.

Chapter Eighteen

Paula Stevens, in the company of her parents, visited St Peter's on Speech Day. Paul had regularly written to her since Arosa and the affection between them had deepened. Paul was waiting for them in the outer quadrangle. As Paula got out of the car Paul held her hand tightly. He held back his desire to embrace and kiss her, which was so strong in him. She in turn held his hand for a long moment and then said, 'Hello Paul – it's lovely to see you.' She glanced at the buildings. 'What magnificent surroundings! It all looks so solid and permanent.'

'Wait until you see the chapel,' he said, while the Stevens walked towards the porter's lodge. 'You look gorgeous, Paula,' he whispered, 'I love you very much. I hope you realise that I want to take you in my arms and kiss you.'

As they were catching up with her parents, she murmured excitedly and quietly, 'I'm hoping Mummy will be asking you to come and stay with us during the summer holidays, so keep your fingers crossed.'

'If she doesn't, I'll ask myself,' he grinned.

The day was a happy one, with a cloudless blue sky, and the distant South Downs forming a rich green backcloth to the black, grey and white flint stone of the school. The parents and visitors tried to outdress each other. The women wearing creations which would only be worn for this one day. Within two years many of these people would be thousands of miles apart and the skies above, although still blue, would be filled with the noise of air battles. The quadrangles of the school would be littered with many spent cartridge cases from the guns of the aircraft above.

Paul took the Stevens and Paula round the school – the house rooms, the studies, the dormitories and the beautiful chapel. Until that day he had not realised how dignified and imposing his school of St Peter's was. The Stevens were full of praise for everything they saw. In the afternoon the annual school cricket match with the Old Boys gave Paul his first chance of being alone with Paula. They had left her parents comfortably installed in deckchairs in front of the pavilion. Paul walked Paula round the boundary of the playing fields.

'Paula, I never imagined that I would have the opportunity of speaking to the girl I love at St Peter's.'

They were walking slowly and pretending to watch the cricket.

'Paul, it is right, isn't it? I mean, you and me. We're not exactly very old,' she laughed. 'I find that I just can't stop thinking about you and—'

'Paula,' he interrupted, 'of course it's right.' At that moment two of the senior boys walked past them.

'Nice day,' said one.

'All right for you,' said the other. They wandered on, grinning. Paula did look very lovely.

Paul went on talking. 'I heard from my uncle a few days ago. It looks as if he's come to live in England for a while.'

'Oh Paul, that's marvellous! It means we can now see a lot of each other during the holidays. Why didn't you tell me sooner?'

'It's not as straightforward as that.' His young face looked puzzled. A wicket fell and they heard the clapping. By now they had reached the far end of the boundary. 'Paula, I've got something very important to tell you, only I don't know whether this is the right moment.'

'You'll only find that out by telling me.' A soft breeze blew from the west and caught her hair with its gentle touch. She looked at his troubled face – she had always seen it laughing and happy before. She felt an uneasiness and was disturbed by his expression. He still said nothing.

'Paul, no secrets now.' She tried laughing, but he didn't. Instead he blurted out, 'I don't want to stay in this country much longer, and Paula, it's not that I don't like it, it's that I love somewhere else much more.'

For a flash she saw herself as the wife of a colonial official, or stationed in some outlandish corner of the British Empire. She didn't like what she saw in her mind. She had just read a book about India which she had loathed. But she said, 'Daddy told me that your school had a reputation for sending its boys into the Colonial Service, so it's not surprising that you feel that way. What is it? The Indian Army?'

'Good Lord, no,' and before he could stop, he hurried on, 'it's Germany.'

He looked sideways at her to see her reaction.

'Well,' she said with a relieved look, 'what's so difficult about telling me that? For a moment I thought you were going to wave the Empire flag! I've just read a book about life in India; from what I read in it, married life out there doesn't get much of a chance to succeed.' She suddenly blushed at what she had said.

Paul looked happy again, and was quick to follow her remark about marriage.

'Paula, who said anything about marriage?' and then he smiled and added, 'You're right, of course! We will get married.' He was overjoyed at her acceptance. But he said, 'You know the only females we see during term time are the college maids. They're not exactly oil paintings, but it does mean that most of the boys here are very immature when it comes to girls.' He paused and Paula didn't like what he was saying. She waited for him to continue, turning her back to him to watch the cricket. A lone cloud crossed the sun's path and another wicket fell.

Paul continued from behind her, 'What I'm trying to say is that on the continent and of course in Germany boys and girls see a lot more of each other and mix much more than over here and therefore are able to be more certain in their choice of the girl they want by their side for all their lifetime.'

She didn't turn to look at him but said, 'Does that mean that you've had lots of other girls before me?'

'Yes, but I've never been in love with one before, in the way I feel about you. And, Paula, don't look round, because if you do I'll kiss you and then there will be hell to pay with most of the school looking this way. But I do love you terribly and I know that I'll always need you by my side.'

She turned round and faced him. 'You will have to avoid kissing me, but Paul, I do love you, oh so much. Just as much as you do me. Let's walk on slowly while you tell me more about Germany. I must warn you, though, not to talk about the country to my father. For some reason best known to himself he often says that he can't stand the Germans.'

'That brings me to a very important point, Paula. I won't talk about the country and when you meet my uncle Heide you mustn't talk to him about it either.' He then gave her a very brief story of his life so far, which she thought terribly exciting. They reached the end of the boundary near the school and retraced their steps. Halfway back to the pavilion Paula had a good idea of Paul's background, and then he started to speak of Germany.

'This country has got the wrong impression of Hitler – he really is a great man, Paula, and what is more important, he is a big supporter of youth.' He gave her a most romantic picture of the Youth Movement's activities and she listened eagerly to his ardent and fervent words. She was completely swept away by his description of the Germany he knew and the one which would soon develop. Then she heard him say, '...and Paula, you must not talk about this to anyone. The older people in this country don't understand the social revolution going on in Germany—' and then they were nearing the pavilion and they saw her mother get up from her chair and come towards them.

They halted and turned to watch the cricket.

'And Paula,' he leaned his head on one side towards her and whispered, 'will you marry me one day?' When she said 'Yes' it seemed the most natural thing in the world.

A week before the end of the summer term Seebohm wrote to Paul giving him instructions that he was to return to Germany towards the end of August. He could stay with his traitorous uncle for some weeks in England then he must leave. The German ship *Heilbronn* would be at Tilbury for three days in August from the 26th to the 29th. He did not have to worry about money as the question of the fare did not arise. Paul was to report to Seebohm's Hamburg office immediately the ship docked at the port. Paul acknowledged receipt of these instructions. The same day he sat for the Civil Service Commissioner Examination, which it was essential to pass for entry into the Royal Military Academy, Sandhurst.

Chapter Nineteen

Heide attended the end-of-term service at St Peter's. It was Paul's last day at the school. The German sat throughout the service next to the headmaster. He had lunched at his house and the meal had been dominated by talk of Colonel Bedford's trial and sentence, which had been announced the previous day.

Raiment had spoken of the unfairness of the trial and called on Heide to express his opinion.

'I have not been in Germany since Bedford's arrest. If he was spying, then of course the likelihood of arrest is an occupational hazard and I imagine that he was prepared for this to happen. But it is a double blow for you, Headmaster, for I know how much he loved his old school and how proud he was to be associated with any scheme launched to further its prosperity.'

'Is there no way of finding out what's going to happen to him, Herr Heide?'

'That is most unlikely.'

'Is there no one you know who might be able to help?'

Heide thought carefully before replying. 'No, under the present regime in my country it is impossible to do anything like that.'

'But surely, Herr Heide, there must be someone you know? You had a distinguished record in the last war fighting for your country. Could you not do something?'

What nonsense the man was talking. The English had no idea of the life being led by any opponents of Hitler's party. Raiment was only one of millions living in such ignorance.

Heide said, 'Not only is there nothing I can do, there is nothing anyone can do. There is a reign of terror in my country. The Germans put Hitler in power because there seemed no alternative. Now many of them want to get him out of power but it's hopeless to attempt it.' He put his knife down. 'And yesterday I sought political asylum from your government. Had I not done that, the German embassy in London could have got me merely by saying that I was wanted for criminal charges in Germany.'

Raiment expressed his sympathy. It was best not to talk at such a moment. Heide went on telling Raiment about the conditions in Germany. 'In a nutshell,' he continued, 'the reason I have been forced to leave my country stems from my political opposition to the Nazis.'

Raiment replied, 'If that is a criminal offence then the rule of Hitler is supreme. How wicked he must be.'

'But surely, Headmaster, you have heard and read about the persecution of his opponents? This country and America already have many of our refugees.'

'Yes, we know of these events, but the only way to stop them would be war against Germany. I do not think that public opinion in this country is sufficiently roused yet. Certainly it is not in America.'

'In Germany at the moment,' continued Heide, 'there are Germans who are doing all they can to bring about a change. In my small way I have even tried to help your government. If action isn't taken soon then the whole continent of Europe may come under the control of the Nazis!'

'We are a people that cannot be rushed,' replied Raiment. 'We are, of course, distrustful of extremes in government, but I repeat, short of war, I cannot see what help we can give.'

'If you leave it that long you may never have the chance to recover.'

Raiment paused and said, 'We still believe in ourselves, Herr Heide, even if we believe in nothing much else, and as for being too late, we are blessed with a certain genius for recovery.'

During the chapel service the chaplain had given a lengthy prayer for Colonel Bedford. At least, thought Heide, the man's arrest had highlighted the Nazis and what they were doing. He felt curious to know whether the colonel had betrayed him. He couldn't conceive how the Nazis had been able to act so quickly against him. He saw Paul in the prefect's pews and he suddenly felt very proud of him. He, at any rate, would now stay in England and his link in the Nazi chain would be broken. He stood up for the traditional last hymn of term. The last four lines of the Christian hymn were bellowed by five hundred voices as the organ swelled to the climax:

> *I will not cease from mental fight,*
> *Nor shall my sword sleep in my hand,*
> *Till we have built Jerusalem,*
> *In England's green and pleasant land'.*

Paul's bedroom was next door to his uncle's at the London hotel. As soon as he was on his own he phoned Paula.

'There you are,' he said, 'I told you – here I am in London—'

'Paul, it's grand to hear you.' Her voice sounded very formal.

'Is there someone else near you? Say yes if that's so.'

'Yes, that's right,' Paula said.

'OK, then here goes. I love you more than anyone else in the world.'

'I'm so glad you had a nice break.'

They both laughed at each other down the phone.

'How did you get on in the exam for Sandhurst?' she asked.

'Oh, fine I think – I hope. Can you come round here for dinner tonight?'

'I'd love to Paul, hold on.' She asked her mother. 'Paul,' she then said, 'that would be lovely. Mummy says you're to come here and collect me.'

'Will do – I'll be there about seven.'

Paul's knowledge of London was very limited, consisting entirely of what he had seen from a taxi on the way to and from Victoria and Liverpool Street stations on the journeys from Hamburg to his Sussex school. Heide had suggested the dinner for he wanted to meet Paula. He asked Paul if he would like him to go with him to collect the girl.

'No, Uncle, I can manage – provided you give me the money for the taxi.' He wanted to keep the Stevens away from his uncle for as long as possible. It would be impossible to keep them off the subject of Germany. He could cope with Paula and his uncle on their own, but with three adults... He only had a few weeks to persuade Paula to marry him and go with him to Germany.

He walked out of the hotel, declining the doorman's offer to get a taxi for him, and wandered up Park Lane towards Marble Arch. He thought there was something nice about London. He admired the tall buildings and liked the park opposite. He didn't like the crowds of people though, and wondered it if was always like this. He didn't know it was rush hour.

Near the top of Park Lane he waved to a taxi.

'Westminster Mansions, please,' he said to the driver. He sat back in the seat and then moved forward to its edge. 'I like the look of London,' he called out to the driver.

'It's all right, guv, but not much fun driving in this bleedin' traffic.'

'Is it always like this?'

'Blimey no, I'd pack in if it was. This is the rush hour, when all these perishers are on their way home from work. It's generally bad at this time.'

'Have you always been a taxi driver?' asked Paul.

'Yes, since the war. It's not a bad life, meet lots of people you know. Foreigners as well. They're all right, too, except the bloody Germans.'

'What's wrong with them?'

'What's right with 'em you mean.' Paul then sat back in his seat listening to the driver's forthright views. How could this man possibly form an opinion of his people, Paul wondered. The only ones he had met were in his cab for a short time or else were soldiers he had seen in trenches opposite him during the war.

Paula liked Heide from the moment she saw him. He seemed so friendly and polite.

'So you're the young lady that Paul speaks so much about – I see why now,' he had said to her when they met. Heide took an instant liking to the girl as well. He soon discovered that her attractiveness was matched by her intelligence and sensitive nature. They looked a handsome couple sitting opposite him in the restaurant.

Paul spent most of the meal keeping the other two off the subject of Germany. This was easily done by talking about St Peter's and Sandhurst. Gaps in the conversation were filled by talk of Arosa, and then while they drank coffee Paula said to Heide, 'I have heard that you are living more or less permanently in England now, Mr Heide?'

'Yes, that's so.'

Paul quickly added, 'It's because you have so much business over here that you felt you might as well stay in this country for a while – that's so, isn't it, Uncle?'

Heide didn't want Paul to look foolish in front of Paula – so he said, 'That's partly true, but not the whole story.'

Paul sought to change the subject. 'The other day, Paula, I was thinking of that little railway that goes from Chur up the mountains to Arosa. Do you remember how steep the track was in places? And how we wondered if the train would get past the snowdrifts forming on the line?'

'Do I just!' she said. 'I remember even more vividly the first time I went down that slope behind the hotel on skis – I thought I'd never stop!'

'You didn't – that snow bank stopped you!'

They were laughing. Outwardly Heide joined in, but he felt he must say more about Germany to Paula. He had the idea at the back of his mind that Paul might listen to her more than he would listen to him. He abruptly said, 'You were asking me the reasons I left Germany, Paula.'

Paul cut in. 'That's all answered, Uncle. I'd like to show Paula the games room here.' He stood up.

'Wait a moment, Paul, I haven't quite finished my answer to Paula.' Paul sat down again, Paula had made no move to leave the table. 'The main reason for my renouncing Germany – for that's what I have done, I haven't just left the country, I may never go back – is because at the moment I can see nothing but tyranny and oppression from its present rulers. Should the government change then I would hope to return. One doesn't leave one's country of birth without a very solid reason in mind.'

The stupid man, thought Paul. *What an unhappy man*, thought Paula. She said, 'Mr Heide, I think I can see what you mean and I feel very sad for you,' and then, seeing Paul's frown, she went on, 'Don't you think, though, that perhaps the country will develop into a much better one? Paul has told me of the improvements that are taking place.'

Before Heide could reply Paul started to talk in a loud voice. 'My uncle only sees the country though the eyes of an old man.'

'Paul, that's very rude,' Paula suddenly blurted out. They were moving towards their first quarrel.

'I didn't mean it to be rude – it's just the truth that's all.' His eyes looked hard. 'Uncle, do you mind now if we just have a wander?'

'No, of course not. There will be some dancing here soon, so don't be too long.'

Paul took Paula's arm and guided her out of the restaurant towards the lounge. They sat down at the only unoccupied table in the centre of the room.

For a while neither spoke. 'I thought I told you not to discuss Germany with my uncle,' he then said angrily, and Paula retorted, 'If you want me to live there with you one day I see no harm in asking someone like your uncle who has lived there all his life.'

'If that's how you feel about breaking a promise, then I'll know what your word is worth in future.' He suddenly stopped and looked at her. He had an overwhelming feeling to stop the row that was developing. His mouth was dry; he didn't want to argue with her. He had felt like this at school just before he received punishment for breaking a rule. He wanted to say he was sorry.

'I cannot recall making such a promise. If I did, then that was very silly of me, for why shouldn't I ask people about Germany?'

'I warned you that older people have the wrong impression of Germany.' He went on, 'If you really loved me you would do what I say. My uncle is completely biased against the Nazis because they're too progressive for him. It's the same with lots of other Germans.'

She saw a chance to lower the temperature between them both, but she said, 'Could it be that perhaps you are wrong and your uncle and the others are right? In any case, Paul, you are British. You may well go to Sandhurst. There's lots of time to think about where and how you're going to live. For the life of me, I just cannot see how you are ever going to live in Germany.' And then she made the mistake of laughing at him. 'A British Officer living in Germany! I can't see you staying in the British Army for long.'

'You're a bloody fool, Paula.' Paul bitterly regretted the

remark as soon as he had said it. She had stood up. Paul's words had been heard by people at nearby tables and they were staring at them both.

'If you will get me a taxi I can find my own way home.'

'Paula, I'm sorry – I – I don't know what made me say that. Please, forgive me.' Still standing, she said, 'Perhaps it is something you've been taught in the Youth Movement.'

They both heard Heide's voice.

'Hello you two – I thought you were going to the games room?'

'Mr Heide, I'm afraid I've got to go home now.'

'Yes, Uncle, Paula doesn't feel too well. I'll take her home.'

Oh no, Mr Heide, I feel fine.

'All right, Paula,' said Paul viciously, 'good night.' And he swaggered out of the lounge.

Heide tried to reason with Paula. 'This sort of thing often happens between people. It will be all right in the morning. Shall I go and bring him back?'

'No, thank you, Mr Heide. I must go home.'

Heide saw the tears in her eyes and said, 'I'll take you, my dear.'

When the cab arrived at Westminster Mansions, Heide said, 'I think it best not to meet your parents tonight. It's quite late, so they won't think you've come back too early. It may be best not to say anything about the row.'

As she left him by the cab, he could see the tears rolling down her cheeks. The cab driver said to him as they drove away, 'Nice girl you had with you, mister.'

'Yes, very nice – my nephew's girlfriend.'

The dirty old man, thought the driver. Heide's cigar had gone out. There was a trail of ash down his lapel. *The sooner Paul is at Sandhurst the better* he said to himself. Paul wouldn't answer the door when Heide knocked. He went to bed but was unable to sleep.

Chapter Twenty

Heide and Paul met at breakfast. There was silence until the boy said, 'Did you see her home all right last night, Uncle?'

'Yes, Paul. She was very upset.'

'I see. I didn't want that to happen. It wouldn't have done if Germany hadn't been discussed.'

'Paul, you must realise that Germany and us have nothing in common now. Can't you see that I have left the country?' He paused. 'As far as you are now concerned it must be forgotten. You are English and about to enter Sandhurst. The ties of your education are much stronger than the Youth Movement. You have managed all these years to keep your feelings regarding the Movement below the surface when you've been in this country. Now make the supreme effort and get it out of your system for ever—'

Paul made no reply. He reached for more toast.

Heide was encouraged by Paul's silence and repeated, 'Get it out of your system! I know you've had your good times with the young Germans, but now you are a man and the picture changes when that occurs.'

Paul continued to stay silent.

'You are all I've got now, Paul. It could be that one day we can live in Germany again, but until then I know you'll accept the situation – for my sake, perhaps?'

'Perhaps,' Paul said. 'If you will excuse me, Uncle, I am going to try and phone Paula.'

Heide looked at the boy disappearing out of the restaurant. Had he changed? Heide reflected on the article he had recently read by a psychologist, where he learned that the latest theory

THE TRIUMPH OF LOVE AND LIBERTY

was that the most formative and influential years were between the ages of ten and fifteen. He could, however, be sure of one thing: Paul would no longer be in Germany.

It took two days of persistent phone calls before Paul was able to speak to Paula. She replaced the receiver every time she heard his voice. It was her mother who made her relent.

'Paula, you must get used to having bad times as well as good. I have always liked Paul, and though your father once disapproved, as you know, he has changed his mind since finding out he went to St Peter's. What happened the other night?'

'We had a row, and Paul was exceedingly rude to me.'

'Well, for heaven's sake make up your mind one way or the other, because I can't stand that phone ringing much more,' Mrs Stevens said in a final tone of voice. 'I'll speak to him next time if you don't.'

Since the quarrel, Paula had been thinking about Germany and in addition reading of the Nazis' rise to power in a book she had found in her father's study. Written by an eminent German surgeon, now exiled in America, having been forced to leave the country because of his Jewish blood, the book had turned Paula away from the version Paul had given her of Germany.

And now today, the *Picture Post*, the weekly pictorial journal, had published pictures showing members of the Nazi Youth Movement breaking up shops in a busy German street, and in the same town a group of the same vandals burning a pile of books well over ten feet high. The photographer had highlighted one of the titles. It was the Bible. The article writing up the photos was headed 'The four freedoms – what price the Nazis now?'

She had just finished reading this when the phone rang.

'Answer the phone,' shouted her mother from the kitchen, 'and if it's Paul, for pity's sake speak to him.'

She sensed it was him as she lifted the receiver.

'Paula, now please don't ring off – quickly say you won't.'
'Paul,' she said, 'what's the point?'
'Every point in the world,' he said. 'I'm sorry for what I said to you the other night. It was said on the spur of the moment. Can't you see that?' And then he whispered, 'In any case, I love you so much and I feel very miserable.'
'I don't exactly feel happy, Paul,' she faltered.
'Well then, it's just damn silly being like this. Can I come round and see you this afternoon?'
'Yes, OK, Paul,' she found herself saying after a long pause.
He took her to the Tower of London, and by teatime the quarrel had been forgotten.
'Did you hear the Beefeater talking about the Ceremony of the Keys? Let's watch that this evening and then have a meal afterwards.'
'That's a great idea,' Paula quickly agreed.
Later, when the Tower had been safely locked up, they took a taxi to Jermyn Street and found a place where the food wasn't too expensive and the dance floor and band were excellent.
'Paula,' Paul said seriously once the meal had been ordered, 'I think I love you more now than I did before our row. I seem closer to you.'
'Paul, you know I love you – I wouldn't have come out with you today if I didn't.'
'And Paula,' he continued, 'about the other night—'
'We agreed not to talk about that,' she cut in.
'I know, but there is still this problem of my going to Germany one day.' He hesitated. 'Time isn't on our side.'
'Don't be silly, we've got all the time in the world.'
'I wish we had, but we haven't.'
'Oh come on, Paul, let's not spoil the wonderful day we've spent together. Aren't you going to ask me to dance?'
He was a bad dancer, but they moved slowly round the tiny floor, so it didn't matter. Not that she would have worried

– she felt again that there would never be anyone else in the world like him.

Paul made no further mention of Germany that night. The following day the Stevenses took Paula with them for a fortnight's stay with some friends at Bury St Edmunds. Paul phoned her every night. Meanwhile, Heide avoided any talk of Germany in front of Paul. A closer relationship then developed between them – closer than at any other time. During the holidays at Hamburg, Paul had spent so many hours with the Youth Movement that they had seen little of each other. But now, for the first time in his young life, Paul had the glimmerings of appreciation for all the help his foster uncle had given to him. He began to feel a certain doubt, only small, but doubt nonetheless, about going to Germany. Paula was due to return to London on the 22nd of August, leaving him only a few days in which to tell her of his plans before he left.

He started to feel desperately unhappy, and then the event occurred that not only steadied him in his resolution to go to Germany, but at the same time set the seal on his separation from Paula.

The day before he was to see her again he went for a stroll in Hyde Park. He wandered aimlessly along towards the Serpentine and stood to watch a group of people feeding the ducks. And then he heard them speaking German. He moved closer to listen. Among the party of six was a tall angular man whose educated German voice dominated the conversation. Paul suddenly felt gladdened at the sight of them and, choosing the right moment during a lull in the conversation, he went up to the tall man and said in German: 'Good afternoon, sir. I have lived for many years in Hamburg. Although of British nationality, I like to consider myself a German.'

'That is most commendable,' laughed the tall one. 'And what is your name?'

'Paul Heide, sir.'

'And mine is Herr von Ribbentrop.' The man then introduced his companions and added, 'For my sins, I am the Führer's ambassador to this country.'

Paul's next move was second nature to him. 'Heil Hitler,' he said, and raised his arm in the Nazi salute. To the surprise of many Londoners passing by, the delighted Ribbentrop returned the salute, while the rest of the party followed suit.

'You see, my friends,' said Ribbentrop, seeming to be addressing all of Hyde Park, 'our Führer's words and teachings have spread to this fair isle of peace. There can never be another war between us.'

Paul accompanied the party back towards the embassy cars. He gave Ribbentrop a very brief account of his life in Germany, which the Nazi listened to very keenly, and as he got into his car he paused and turned to Paul.

'Did you say your name was Heide?'

'Yes, sir – he's my foster uncle.'

The ambassador's suave and smooth face broadened with a grin.

'You'll no doubt teach him the errors of his ways, young man!'

'I'm not sure of that, sir, but meeting you today has renewed my faith in the power of Germany.' A puzzled but still delighted Ribbentrop got into his car.

On his return to the hotel, Paul did not mention his meeting in the park. But a *Daily Echo* photographer hadn't missed the opportunity to record the scene.

On the front page of the daily paper there was a photo of Paul shaking hands with Ribbentrop and another of the young man giving the Nazi salute. Heide rushed into Paul's bedroom with the paper. He was shaving, and he saw his uncle's face in the mirror.

'Paul, why didn't you tell me about this?' Heide showed him the paper. Paul looked back in the mirror, went on shaving, and then said in a matter-of-fact tone, 'It's a darned good photo, Uncle.'

'Stop shaving and listen to me.' Heide's tone made Paul turn round and face him. 'This is an absolute disgrace for me and for you too. Here you are, not only giving a Nazi salute but also being friendly with a man who represents the people responsible for my eviction from Germany. They are wicked people, Paul, and I forbid you ever to have any more dealings of even the remotest kind with any of them.'

Paul's inner feelings revolted against his uncle's tirade against the Nazis. He wanted to shout him down. His recent thoughts of sympathy for him vanished as he stood up to Heide and said with great control, 'I'm sorry it has upset you so much, Uncle. I won't let it happen again.'

Heide calmed down and then said in a quieter voice, 'Paul, please get the Nazis out of your mind. I worry about you so much at times. You seem to have few friends over here. What happened to the boy you were so friendly with when you first went to St Peter's – John Bright I think he was called?'

'We just seemed to go our separate ways. I worked and played hard at school and found that there was no time to make any deep friendships.'

'All right, Paul, let's forget this argument.' Heide felt old and completely out of touch with the boy's opinions and state of mind. He had rushed into Paul's bedroom intent on punishing him in some way – he hadn't known how – yet here he was a few minutes later, walking out and quietly closing the door behind him.

Paul had wanted to control his feelings. He hadn't wanted to go so far with Paula – she was carried away as much as he was. It was her second day back in London, and when Paul had suggested a day on the river at Richmond she thought there could have been nothing nicer. Although it was the middle of August, the river was not crowded, the day being heavy and overcast. It had been easy to hire the motor launch, with its cabin with two berths in the bows. The tiny galley added to the cosiness, and while Paul steered up river in the direction of Hampton Court, Paula prepared the lunch. They had hired the boat until ten o'clock that evening. Paul hoped that by that time his plan to live in Germany would be fully known to Paula and some means found of getting her out there too.

A few miles from Hampton Court, Paul saw a small island in the middle of the river. Calling to Paula below to come on deck, he steered towards it.

'That looks a great place to anchor for lunch – shall we make for it, Paula?'

'That looks fine, and lunch is just about ready,' she replied.

He secured the bows to the branch of an overhanging willow tree. It had started to drizzle and as he went below, the cosiness of the little saloon made him say, 'Paula, let's close the hatch and stay here for ever,' and then he had taken her in his arms.

She broke away and said, laughing, 'If you think that this gorgeous meal is going to be ruined, you're much mistaken, Mr Heide! Now come on sit down and see what you think of my cooking.'

Later he said, 'If you feed all my wants in such a way, then I shall always be a very happy man with you, Mrs Heide.' She didn't laugh when he called her Mrs Heide. They were sitting opposite each other. He went across and sat beside her.

'Your hair looks beautiful today,' he murmured and then he added, 'darling.'

She turned towards him, 'And what about my eyes?' They were sparkling and full of love.

'They look a kind of blue, and yet I can see some green there as well.' He passed his fingers through her hair and she closed her eyes. He kissed her behind the ears and then across her cheeks until his lips reached her mouth. His hand caressed her back. 'Paul,' she whispered in his ear, 'I love you, I love you. I wish I could find some other words to say but there aren't any, just I love you.'

'There's no need to say anything more than that.'

He took his arms away form her body and lay full length on the bunk. She remained sitting on its edge, her blouse buttoned down the back. His fingers started to undo each one very slowly and Paula just continued to sit, staring in front of her. Through the small porthole she could see the little island. She tried to pretend that this was not happening to her. Paul had undressed her to the waist. He was slowly stroking her breasts and then she groaned, 'No, Paul, no,' but she didn't resist when he gently pulled her down to his side... It started to rain hard.

They had both fallen asleep afterwards. Paula awoke first and awakened him with a kiss. They lay on their backs listening to the rain.

Paul, why do you want to live in Germany?

'When I ask myself that question,' Paul said, 'the same answer always comes to me – because I admire and respect Hitler as a man, because I like the German people, especially the young ones, because Germany is a country of physical contrasts – you know, lots of beautiful lakes and in the south the mountains – but mostly because I think that the country has much greater opportunities for youth than England.'

'But if you do live there, what will you do? What work will you take up?' asked Paula.

'That's not difficult to answer: I shall work for the Nazis in any way that they think I can be of service to the Party.'

She sat up and edged herself to the end of the bunk. She turned to face him.

He said, 'Now don't wander off down there, come on back here.'

'No, Paul, I just want to sit away from you for a while.

I can't think clearly when you're holding me close. I feel we must have a serious chat about your future.' He raised himself on his elbow and looked at her. 'I have been reading a book about the Nazis,' she continued. 'I have also seen some beastly photos of members of your Youth Movement beating innocent people and quite pointlessly burning books that the "Party" doesn't want Germans to go on reading – one of the books was the Bible.'

'I don't know what sort of books you've been reading,' Paul said, 'no doubt anti-Nazi ones supplied by your father. I'm sure the photos you saw were faked,' Paul went on. 'The point is, Paula, that if you had seen the way in which the Jews had bled the country dry for their own purposes, you would realise how important it is for them to be—' He paused; he had nearly said 'liquidated'. '—left out of the scheme of things for Germany. If they cannot accept the necessary reforms essential for the country's recovery then it is only right that they should be expelled.'

'But your uncle is not a Jew and he loves his country, yet he's left.'

'There are other matters concerning him which one day you will discover.' Paul knew that she didn't want to go to Germany. His only hope now lay in getting her out there at a future date. He also realised that he had got to earn money in order to support them both.

He stood up and went over to her. Still standing he caressed her shoulders and said, 'There's one thing I have to know, Paula. If I go to Germany, will you come out to me one day? I will call for you as soon as I'm ready, as soon as I have some money. Will you do that?'

She leaned against him and without looking up, sighed.

'I'm all mixed up about Germany, but if there is one thing that's crystal clear, it's my love for you. I'll come to you wherever you are.'

They kissed for a long time.

When Paul left her that night, he still hadn't told her the date of his departure for Germany.

Chapter Twenty-one

Heide was asleep in the lounge when Paul retuned from Richmond. 'Wake up, Uncle,' Paul said. 'We've had a glorious day. We went on the river to Richmond.'

'I've heard that is a very lovely place. I'm glad you enjoyed it there. As a matter of fact I have been waiting up to see you. I have got to go to Manchester tomorrow on business. I'll be away about a week, for there's a lot to discuss with the manufacturer and I don't want to do it piecemeal. I may be back before a week's out, but it's not likely.'

Paul sat down. When Heide asked him if he'd like a coffee he said he would, and then added, 'Well, I can look after myself.'

Heide continued, 'I have left some money with the manager – ask him when you want some. He'll probably ask you to sign for it. That reminds me, I'm going to open a bank account for you.'

Money, or rather the lack of it, was still much in Paul's thoughts. He said, 'Thank you very much, Uncle.' And then as an idea crossed his mind he added, 'When exactly do I get the money my parents left me?'

Heide was momentarily surprised by Paul's question but then quickly realised that it was only natural the boy should want to know.

'You come into that when you're twenty-one. Not so long to wait now. I wonder where you will be then?' he smiled.

'Probably on the North-West Frontier cursing my luck that I can't get at the money to spend it!' And then, 'I wonder where you will be, Uncle?'

Heide looked serious and said, 'I hope, perhaps, I'll be back in Germany. Who can tell?'

'Uncle, don't let's argue, but I think that you've been wrong about the Nazis all along. If only you could see your way to believing in them again. You did for quite a while...'

Now was the moment to tell Paul. 'When I left Germany, within a matter of hours the house was searched in Hamburg.' Paul couldn't look up at him; he sat with his head bowed, staring into the coffee cup. 'I don't know what they found – for all they knew, I was going back. What I do know is that within a few days of being here in London, the German embassy tried to force the authorities to hand me over to them. They know I haven't always supported them.' He paused, and then went on, 'There was also another matter I cannot discuss with you now, but in any event, I did not want to spend any of my remaining years in a concentration camp, or even worse. I had to ask for political asylum – do you understand that, Paul?'

'Yes, I see. I would like to say more but I can't either.'

'What do you mean, Paul?'

'Oh, nothing, Uncle. Let's just leave it there.' Paul got up from the table. 'Bed for me now.'

'And for me, too.' On the way up in the lift Heide told him he was getting an early train in the morning and would have left the hotel before Paul had breakfast.

Outside Paul's room Heide said, 'Enjoy yourself while I'm away. I expect you'll be seeing a lot of Paula?'

'Yes, yes I will,' Paul said slowly, and then, 'Uncle, I hope you will always think well of me and understand when I do things you sometimes don't approve of.'

'Of course, Paul. None of us ever stops learning. Only, I like to see you going along the right road of life.' They shook hands and said goodnight. They would both recall the last two sentences spoken to each other many times in the years that lay ahead.

Paul left the letter he had written to his uncle at the reception desk of the hotel. He knew it was too long and that he had been unable to express his thoughts in a convincing way but he had been pleased with his last paragraph: 'And so,' he had concluded, 'I must go to Germany. I know that you will be unable to understand me. I only hope that you will be able in your heart to forgive me. I know that I am doing the right thing.'

He told the receptionist that he was staying with friends until his uncle's return. He collected ten of the pound notes left by Heide, and with one large suitcase left the hotel. It was the 29th of August.

He met Paula as arranged near Westminster Mansions. Their coffee in the restaurant went untouched.

'Paul, since you told me of your plans last night, I've been sick with worry about you. Even now I can't believe it's happening.'

'It's the only way for me, darling. I've got to go to Germany, the country's in my blood.' Sometime later, for they just sat looking at each other for a long time, he said, 'I'll get you out there as soon as I can.'

She said, 'What about your uncle? This will kill him.'

Paul said quickly, 'No, he's probably had worse shocks than this. I hope you'll go and see him.'

'Of course I will.' She continued staring at him, still with a look of disbelief. His suitcase by the table brought her back to reality. 'Paul,' she hesitated, 'the thing we did at Richmond. You think it will be all right?'

'What do you mean?'

She looked at the nearby tables and whispered, 'I won't have a baby?'

'No, er, no.' It hadn't occurred to him as being even a remote possibility. 'No, there's no chance of that, is there?'

The question was thrown back to her. 'No, I'm sure you're right, there won't be.' And then, 'I don't know anything about these things.'

'I am certain there's not the slightest need to worry about that. You just concentrate on the day when you'll be joining me.'

Paula went on, 'I have decided to tell my parents tomorrow of your plan. At least to tell them you've gone to Germany.'

'Yes, I suppose you must,' he replied.

'Can I come with you to the station, Paul?'

'I think it best to say goodbye here, Paula. It's best not to prolong goodbyes.' With the assurance that he would be writing to her in the next few days, Paul slowly stood up and said, 'I'm going to ask you to look at that mirror over there. I'm going to kiss you. I will never forget you or let you down, darling. I'll always love you and sooner than we think we'll be together again. Now, look at that mirror and keep on looking at it until I have gone.' He kissed her on the back of her neck for a short moment, then gently squeezed her shoulders and was gone.

She had no idea how long she had been staring at the mirror. The waiter said he wanted to set the table for lunch. She paid him for the coffee and then suddenly ran out into the street. There was no sign of Paul.

Chapter Twenty-two

On his arrival in Hamburg, Paul reported to Seebohm. 'This time you are in Germany for keeps,' the Nazi said to Paul. 'But our original plans have now misfired.'

'What exactly were those plans, Herr Seebohm?'

'We had hoped that you would spend at least a year at Sandhurst. The information you would have obtained about the structure of the British Army, their equipment, and the tactics and strategy of the armed forces would have been of great use to us in the event of a war between Britain and us.'

'What has changed that?' enquired Paul.

'Your uncle's defection to England. We discovered a list of agents working for Britain when Colonel Bedford's room in Berlin was searched. Bedford was a double agent, Paul, working for England yet pretending to be with us.'

Paul was reluctant to believe the news about Bedford, but in an instant he felt a kind of relief that it was not due entirely to him that his uncle's house had been searched. Then he was astonished by the account of Bedford's work both for and against Germany. Seebohm had stopped talking. He lit a cigarette, watching the smoke he exhaled as it drifted to the ceiling. Then he said, 'Your uncle's name was on that list, Paul. He will never return to Germany, and that would have made your return here difficult to accomplish at short notice, too.'

Paul reflected on his present situation: deeply in love with Paula, he had no money and no job, and now Seebohm was inferring that his past three years in England were wasted. He said, 'I want to work for the Nazis. What is the position for me now?'

'Paul you shall work for us. Your education in England will one day be of great value to the Party. At the moment, we consider it necessary for you to join one of our fighting services. Maybe in this field your background can be used to its full advantage.'

'In other words, join the Army?'

'Yes, if that's the service you prefer. You will of course go immediately to an Officers' Training Unit. You will also earn some money.'

Paul replied, 'Would there be a chance of getting my fiancée over to this country?'

'Your fiancée? Who is she?'

'An English girl I know. We love each other and want to marry. She'll come over to Germany when I call for her.'

'This could be arranged, but it would be for you to make the arrangements!' Seebohm smiled. 'Affairs of the heart do not interest me.' He hesitated. 'What does interest me are the moves your uncle may make to force your return to England.'

'There's no hope of that now.'

'Possibly not. In any case, that is another reason why we must, shall I say, lose you for some time in the Army. You will have a month or so here, during which time a small salary will be paid for routine work for the Youth Movement. Your nationality will also be considered.'

Paul was quite indifferent to his nationality. British or German did not matter to him. He was in Germany, and that was the most important thing to him.

Seebohm went on, 'You can communicate with England as and when you wish. This includes your uncle. However, to avoid your true address being known, all correspondence from England should be sent here, care of the Youth Movement Centre. Give them this address. All post will be forwarded to you.'

* * *

On the day in late September 1938 that Chamberlain arrived at Heston airport after seeing Hitler, bringing with him 'peace for our time', life began for Paul in the German Army. On the same day, Paula began to think that she might be pregnant.

The cavalry barracks at Wolfenbüttel, a small town some few miles south of Brunswick, were completed in the early part of 1936. Not a horse could be seen, though, as the barracks were designed for the mechanised age. Through these barracks went the cream of the German cavalry regiments. By the time Paul was posted there the barracks had become the Officers' Training Centre for all the German tank regiments.

Commanded by a Prussian, Colonel Adolf Müller, the barracks became the centre of the new fighting weapon of the German Army, the Panzer Division. It was here, too, that Paul commenced his training on the tank which was destined to sweep the Nazis across Europe – 'Panzer IV'. With its crew of five, and armed with a 75-mm gun and two machine guns, with a cruising speed of 30 mph, the tank was already years ahead of its nearest rivals in 1938. At Sandhurst, training for the cavalry and tank regiments consisted of the cadets riding bicycles, pretending they were tanks.

At Paul's first interview with Colonel Müller, he saluted him in the way he had been trained to in the Youth Movement.

'Heide, we don't Heil Hitler here. Has that not been explained to you?'

'No, sir.'

'Well don't do that again.' Müller was a fine soldier, a good-natured giant of a man, clever and courageous. He loathed any political interference and only tolerated the daily propaganda lectures given by the Nazi SS officer because non-compliance would have meant his immediate dismissal.

'I have a full report of your background, Heide.' He paused. 'I know your uncle well – at least, I knew him well during the war. He is a very brave man. I think today he is even braver.'

Paul had not expected this. He remained silent and stiffly at attention. His new uniform was a perfect fit and he felt very proud.

'Now relax,' said Müller, 'and tell me about yourself.'

Paul then recounted his life in both Germany and England. He gave a brief, though thorough, description of his military training in the Officers' Training Corps at St Peter's.

Müller interrupted him at this stage. 'Was any emphasis laid on the importance of tanks in war?'

'Not really, sir. They were not even considered.'

'You'll find things very different here. Carry on with your story.'

'There's not really much more to say, sir, except that I have come to love this country and that I have a complete trust in the Führer.'

'Yes, of course.' Müller brushed this aside. 'The Nazis are now our leaders. I am a professional soldier and not interested in politics. I see you are now a naturalised German. You will no doubt bear this in mind when you write to your uncle and friends in England.'

'I have no friends in England, sir. There is an English girl I hope one day to marry. That is in the future.'

'I see. You are, of course, right. That is in the future. I would hope that your uncle will hear from you. What does he think of your move here?'

'I've no idea, sir.'

'What do you mean?'

'I just left the country while he was away.'

'Have you written to him yet?'

Paul was at a loss to understand the colonel's interest in his uncle – wasn't the man a traitor? He said, 'No, sir, Herr Seebohm in Hamburg thought it best that I had no contact with him for a time.'

'Heide, I have no objection to you writing to him. Your overseas post will in any case be censored.'

'Thank you, sir, I will remember that.'

'I am correct in saying that your wish to live in this country is based mainly on your high regard for Hitler and the Nazis?'

'Yes, sir.'

'Then I wish you to remember also that here you are first and foremost a German soldier, training to be an officer. Your support for the Nazis is secondary to that.'

It took some days for Paul to recover from his meeting with Müller. Any implications he might have drawn about the colonel's political beliefs were quickly forgotten during the rigorous and intensive training he underwent.

He did not write to Heide. His six letters to Paula had not been answered. But towards the end of October he received his first mail, forwarded from Hamburg. A solitary letter from her father. It was waiting for him on his return to his room, the one he shared with another officer cadet. He sat on his bed, and as he read it his confusion grew. He felt as if a large wave was engulfing him. He read it through, got up, sank into a chair by the window and read it again. His legs felt weak and his whole being reeled. It was as if a hand of steel had seized his heart and crushed it. It was dated three days earlier.

Paul, I do not know if you will ever receive this letter. Your uncle has tried in vain to contact you at the address you have given to Paula in Hamburg. Yes, she has received your letters and so far we have succeeded in preventing her from replying. Perhaps one day, unknown to us, she will do so. In the hope that you get this letter I am writing because I want you to know of the untold misery and unhappiness you have spread. Your selfishness makes me doubt that this letter will have any effect on you. It does, however, help to relieve my feelings.

You are a wretched young man. Since your sudden

departure, your uncle has been very ill. On his return from Manchester, on learning the news about your flight to Germany, he suffered a heart attack, mercifully only a slight one. He has only recently come out of the hospital in London where we have regularly visited him. Even now he doesn't blame you as I do. He lays all the blame at the feet of the Nazis and for the evil morality that they have taught you.

I think otherwise and consider that you are an evil person. St Peter's will wish to forget that you ever attended the school. Since Munich, when this country was at the doorway of another war with Germany, your action in leaving this country seems even more despicable.

Meanwhile, Paula has had recent confirmation from our doctor that she is over two months' pregnant and we know that you are responsible for that. The child will become our responsibility and we can only hope that one day Paula will meet someone who will erase the memory of you finally and for ever. Neither she nor my wife and I ever want to see you again, and if you have a shred of decency left in you, you will stop writing to her. In any event, we will always destroy any letters which you send before opening them. Get out of her life and forget you ever had any upbringing in this country, for you can be sure that it never wants to see you again.

From, Stevens.'

He re-read the letter three times, and then his deep sorrow at receiving such accusations from Paula's father quickly turned to feelings of contempt for the man.

Paul was deeply in love with Paula, but he was also in love with Germany. He wanted the best of all worlds. He was confident in one day proving the rightness of his actions. But at this moment, engulfed in misery, it was Paula's absence that dominated his thoughts.

He felt half persuaded to return to England, and then in a flash realised the stupidity of such an action. He must establish himself in Germany, in the Army, and then find a way of getting her out there to join him. He had no intention of rushing back to England. If Paula's father chose to think the worse of him, that was his problem. Paul tried to look at himself. I'm a resolute, realistic and tenacious young man. That is what he thought he saw.

Paula would know and understand. He remembered how she had promised to wait until he called for her.

Paul lay still on his bed and then sat up and tore Stevens' letter to pieces. He paced up and down his room and found that he desperately wanted to talk to someone.

He suddenly made for the door and, slamming it hard, ran to the orderly room and to the startled sergeant on duty, requesting an interview with Colonel Müller 'as soon as possible'.

Chapter Twenty-three

'I am sorry to hear that you have had bad news from England, Heide.' Müller had arranged to see Paul the morning after he had received the letter from Stevens. Müller could see that the man was emotionally disturbed. 'You had best tell me what has happened,' he continued.

Paul had spent a restless night – his first thought on waking had been about Paula. He wanted to see and comfort her. Stevens had made no mention of the girl's state of mind. He was certain that she still loved him and that, given the chance, she would come to him in Germany. He told Müller of the contents of the letter.

'As I see it, Heide, you have no choice in the matter. There is of course no hope of going to England. Had you remained in England there would have been the same problem with your girl – er, with your fiancée.' Müller was worried lest the man's training would suffer as a result of Stevens' letter.

'My only concern, sir, is for Paula. I suddenly realise that the situation is one that I should have anticipated. It was the shock of the letter that has tormented me.'

Müller said helpfully, 'In that case, it is a question of accepting the situation, working hard here, and then at a later date making an attempt to get this girl of yours over here. But as I said to you the other day, you are now German and in Germany's Army. Your only cure for the problem you have created is work – the cure of work. There is nothing more that can be said.'

Paul smartly saluted the colonel and returned to the gunnery lecture room. On the way he wondered if he would ever see

Paula again. If only he could get a letter from her, just to confirm how she felt about him.

That evening he told his roommate Richard Walldern not only of the letter but also the story of his young life. Walldern was the only son of a doctor whose successful practice in Bad Harzburg was reflected by his beautiful house just outside the town on the lower slopes of the Harz mountains. His father had wanted his son to carry on the family tradition and qualify as a doctor of medicine. Richard's experience in the Youth Movement had prevented that happening. The glamour attached to an officer of the German Army had dominated his mind since the age of fourteen. The prospect of any other career had never entered his head.

The same age as Paul, Richard was much the same height and build, though one of them was blue-eyed, the other grey, one clean shaven, the other with a small moustache. One at the moment happy, the other in despair.

'What the hell can I do now?' Paul asked.

'For one thing, you can cheer up – you'll have me as depressed as you if you don't. And for another, you can forget about Paula. There are plenty of girls over here. Just wait until you are commissioned – you can have any girl you want then.'

'I have no desire to want another girl. You, Richard, may find it hard to believe, but there will never be anyone else for me – just Paula, that's who I want.'

'If you came to stay with me at home you would find someone else within a matter of minutes.'

'You're wrong there, Richard, but that does raise an interesting point. Can I cadge a holiday with you this coming Christmas?'

'Yes, of course, Paul. I was going to ask you anyway.'

'I feel a bit better now, especially as you know of my problems. Is it possible to ski in the Harz mountains?'

'Yes, and with any luck there should be plenty of snow by then. Now I suggest that we get down to studying our gunnery lecture notes. I want to pass successfully even if you don't.'

'It's strange to think,' said Paul, 'that I might have been at Sandhurst now.'

'Just as well you aren't – you want to be on the winning side next time, don't you?'

Before Paul went to sleep he wrote another letter to Paula. Two hours previously in England, she had managed to sneak out and post one to him.

Paul could not know what had happened to his mind or the split that his education in England and his membership of the Youth Movement had created in him. Until his meeting with Paula he regarded those of her sex as playthings. He had been taught by the Youth Movement that a young girl who was not prepared to be a mother as quickly as possible was 'lacking in her sense of social duty'. He had even seen advertisements in the Hamburg papers of girls stating their willingness to become mothers and their wish to meet healthy young men. Nazi professors advised that 'to insist upon marriage before motherhood was an outdated notion'. He knew that from the age of sixteen a German girl found the path of motherhood was made easy for her. When the child was born it was left to be brought up in one of the state nursery schools, where Hitler's 'children' were trained to the desired ends. The Nazis had made no allowance for feelings of love and for the great effect this strong human emotion can have on the minds of men and women.

St Peter's had not been able to displace Paul's contempt for Christianity. He still knew the last verse of the song taught by the Youth Movement many years before:

HUGH FRANKS

> *We've given up the Christian line*
> *For Christ was but a Jewish swine*
> *As for his mother, what a shame*
> *Cohen was her maiden name*

And yet, for Paul, his girl in England had meant, and still meant, everything. St Peter's had succeeded in finding a small place at the back of his mind that was reserved for thinking of others. This, and his love for Paula, made him want her by his side. It was this force which kept him writing to her.

He immediately recognised the writing on the envelope. In his eagerness to open the letter he tore a large piece off the top of the first page.

> *Darling Paul*
> *I know that father has written to you. Today was the first opportunity I have had to write to you. I have only been able to read your early letters and so I have no idea where you are or what you are doing. I must tell you first that I am well and I pray to God that you are too.*
> *For a while after you had left I was completely lost. I still pray every night that the day will soon come when I will be able to join you, for I love you very dearly and cannot imagine life without you. Our child will be born next May. Oh Paul I get so frightened sometimes, wondering how this is all going to end.*
> *My parents never want me to see you again, but I don't hate them for this. I think we must both understand their feelings, and Mummy in particular has been extremely kind and thoughtful towards me. Daddy has made an arrangement with the postman whereby it is impossible for me to ever receive any letters from you. My parents*

watch me continually, so I do not have the opportunity to write.

Your uncle is now in much better health. I have seen him once or twice but always with Mummy or Daddy. He doesn't think badly of you, Paul, but he seems to blame himself for the thing you have done. A month or so ago the Daily Echo got hold of a story about you. They followed it up and then they remembered the time you met Ribbentrop in Hyde Park. They made a big splash about it, particularly just after Munich. They interviewed your uncle and the story got printed on the front page! It was all about Hitler's Youth Movement and the effect it can have on young people. They also interviewed the headmaster at St Peter's, Mr Raiment. I wasn't able to see the article, but heard my parents talking about it.

Paul, when am I going to see you? How are you going to get in contact with me? I will wait for ever if necessary, but just try and find some way of seeing me. I pray to God that you receive this letter and I don't know when I will be able to write again. Your uncle has made many efforts to find you but the German embassy here never seems to pass on any information about you. He's had an interview with our Foreign Minister but nothing concrete came out of it.

I had better stop – my darling Paul I love you so much. I will never marry anyone else and will wait for you, but try and make that meeting soon.

Yours always, Paula

Chapter Twenty-four

Paul enjoyed his Christmas leave at Bad Harzburg with the Wallderns. It had snowed a week before and the two young men skied every day. In the evenings Richard would disappear. He tried to persuade Paul to go out with him but he never succeeded. Paul spent most evenings with the Wallderns – the doctor had visited England many times and had a high regard for the country. He also had little regard for Hitler, but in line with many liberal-minded Germans, was very guarded in the words he used to criticise the regime.

'Have you any regrets?' Walldern enquired one evening to Paul, towards the end of Paul's leave, 'about the choice you have made?'

'You mean my choice of country? None whatsoever, except, of course, not being able to see Paula.' Then he went on, 'I am very proud of my German nationality. I hope, though, that there is not a war. I don't think that will happen, do you, Herr Doctor?'

Paul had quickly returned to the German characteristic of paying excessive veneration to rank.

'The Führer has certainly stated many times that he has no wish to start a war.' Walldern looked at Paul closely and went on, 'The trouble is the rest of the world. Will it stand by and allow us to get what we want without trying to stop us?'

'The Führer has stated time and time again that he has no more territorial claims to make in Germany,' said Paul. 'We must believe this – I certainly don't want a war.'

'Why did you join the Army, Paul?'

'I have always been interested in the services, and was so in England. The Party advised me that this was the best course for me to adopt, and I willingly obeyed it. The day may come when I shall be able to help the Führer by working in a civilian job. I don't mind much either way, as long as I'm over here. I feel confident that my future here is full of promise. In England no one seems to get anywhere until they are well over fifty. Hitler told us repeatedly that we, the young, are to be the awakeners of the new world that he is creating for us alone.'

A very bad case of Nazism, diagnosed Walldern. *I must be careful what I say*, he thought. His phone rang.

'Yes, Dr Walldern speaking. I am very sorry to hear that, Frau Hofer. Yes – yes, of course. I'll be over right away.'

'Paul, I must go out to see a patient immediately. I don't know when my wife will be back. She's somewhere in Goslar visiting friends. You'll be on your own – would you like to come with me?'

'Yes, very much. Perhaps I can help?'

'Come then, we must hurry. I'll tell you about it in the car.'

On the way to the Hofers' house, Walldern suddenly regretted taking Paul. He hadn't thought the matter out sufficiently. He said to Paul, 'Herr Hofer is an old friend of mine as well as a patient. He runs a small though successful factory just outside Goslar. His brother, Walter, is, or more exactly was, vice-president of the Senate of Danzig.' The level-crossing gate in the middle of the town came down and Walldern stopped. 'That always happens when I'm in a hurry. Yes, now, where was I? Oh yes, Hofer's brother in Danzig. It seems that there has been some sort of trouble in Danzig with the man's family, and his brother Walter is very upset about its outcome – they are very close to each other.'

A train stopped at the crossing and the steam from its engine's sides gushed out, enveloping the car.

'I believe,' continued Walldern, 'that the trouble is in some way connected with the Nazis.' He looked across at Paul – the steam was blotting out everything and Paul was peering through the windscreen, at that moment trying to look out.

Paul said, 'I can't see a thing.' He sat back in his seat and, without turning to Walldern, continued, 'Perhaps I should not come in with you.'

'That might be for the best – unless you promise to say nothing of what you hear?'

'Suits me, Herr Doctor.' And still looking ahead, he added, 'I promise.'

Frau Hofer had taken her husband to the bedroom. 'It's good to see you – thank you for coming so quickly,' she said on opening the front door. 'I've taken him upstairs to his room. He has stopped crying, but he's still on the verge of hysteria.'

'I'll go up to him. By the way, this is a friend of Richard's who is staying with us for his leave, Paul Heide.'

Walldern went upstairs. 'Please, sit down,' she said to Paul. Paul liked Frau Hofer if only because she strongly resembled Hilda. He said as much to her. She grinned feebly and said, 'That's the first time I've smiled for days.'

'I'm sorry to hear about your husband, Frau Hofer. I hope he'll soon be well.'

'Thank you – he's had a great shock. Very bad news about his brother.'

'What's happened? Has he had an accident?'

'No.' She paused. 'No, the poor man has been sent to the concentration camp at Sachsenhausen.' She stood up and walked over to the window. She pulled one of the long curtains aside and, holding onto its edge, as if for support, looked out onto the garden. 'Last summer he came here for a holiday.' She seemed to be talking aloud to herself. 'He loved climbing and spent many days with my husband in the mountains. They've always been very close to each other. I used to be quite jealous. He is one of the nicest men I have met – kind, considerate, and. after his love for his family, a Germany living in peace was his one interest in life.'

Paul sat looking at her and followed her with his eyes as she crossed the room. She had left the curtain pulled back.

'I'm sorry, I haven't asked you if you would like a drink.'

'Please, I'd love a beer.'

As she left the room Paul got up and walked over to the window. Frau Hofer came back in and walked over to him with the drink. She handed it to him and, standing by his side, looked out with him into the night.

'Thank you, Frau Hofer. You are not drinking?'

She walked over to the fireplace and warmed her hands from the gentle heat of the smouldering logs.

'It's a cold night. I'm sorry that I had to call the doctor out.'

'He was only too ready to come as quickly as he could. I came with him as I thought the snow might give him trouble on the roads.' Paul joined her by the fireplace and, putting his glass on the little coffee table by the fireside, said, 'Why was he sent to Sachsenhausen?'

'Why is anyone being sent to such places? Why are there such places?' She swung round and faced Paul, her face twisted with rage. 'I'll tell you why!' Her voice rose to a high pitch. 'It's because the Nazis are in power. They're evil men, wicked men. I'll tell you, these days I'm ashamed to be a German woman.'

Paul felt confused by the outburst. The woman still glared at him; she no longer bore any resemblance to Hilda. She had a look of intense dislike as she asked him, 'Are you a Nazi?'

He was for a moment thrown off his balance. He was staggered and a little frightened by the look on her face.

'I am a German.'

'Are you a Nazi?' she persisted.

'I am a Nazi – I am proud to be one,' Paul said as his courage returned. 'I could have remained an Englishman, but of my own free will I changed.'

'You must be mad, young man,' she said, but her face showed a more relaxed expression. 'Would you like to know why my brother-in-law has been arrested and sent to this camp?'

'I was going to ask you.'

'I'll tell you why,' she said, speaking quickly, 'it was because he had the courage to speak out against this terrible government. He tried to say what thousands of Germans want to say but dare not for fear for themselves and families.'

Paul didn't want to listen – he moved away from her, but she followed him to the windows. He stood there with his back to her, looking out of the window. He wanted the doctor to come down and for them to get out of the house.

Frau Hofer stood a yard or so behind him and addressed her words to the back of his neck. 'And I'll tell you why he was finally put away. It was because his own son betrayed him.' Paul suddenly thought of his uncle. She went on, 'There was much, oh so much, that Walter disliked about the Nazi programme, but he accepted the position at Danzig in the hope of directing the movement towards peaceful ends, as many thousands have done.'

She paused to let that sink it and then went on, 'He discovered that his son was responsible for the pregnancy of a young girl. It happened at a Youth Movement camp. He gave the boy a thrashing. His son denounced him by telling the Nazis, and that's why he's been sent to the camp.' Paul turned to look at her. She gazed at him and said in a quieter voice, 'The Nazis awarded a decoration to the boy.'

Paul said nothing and just stared at her. He wished she would stop but she continued, 'Young girls have been turned into so many breeding beasts. Young boys have been taught that it's right and smart – yes, and patriotic – to fornicate.

You must be a proud young man to be associated with such a fine party,' she sneered.

'You have been doing all the talking, Frau Hofer. All I will say is that it would appear that your brother-in-law got what he deserved.'

As she smacked him heavily across the face, Walldern entered the room. 'Frau Hofer,' he gasped. She turned and ran to him, her face already swimming with tears. Walldern held her arms.

'How is he?' she whispered.

'Much better – I've given him a sedative. I'll come and see him tomorrow.' He paused and said, 'You take these tablets too, and go on up to him now.'

The doctor led her to the stairs and watched her climb them slowly. He went back into the room.

'Come on, Paul, we can go now.'

In the car Walldern said, 'What happened?'

'Oh, she just got very upset. I said something that seemed to annoy her and she lashed out at me.'

Walldern was glad that Richard and Paul were going back to Wolfenbüttel in the morning. He got the truth of what occurred from Frau Hofer the next evening.

Chapter Twenty-five

As the year 1939 dragged on towards its inevitable climax in September, Heide lived out its misery in London. He had read the news with despair when in March the Nazi troops invaded Czechoslovakia in flagrant violation of the terms of the Munich Conference. He could see that his people were catching Hitler's sickness as if it were a virus.

His business continued to prosper though he began to detect a certain coldness from some of his associates. Since the day of his arrival in London no contact had been made with the espionage agency and he was thankful to be left alone. The Anglo-German Society had long since vanished, its members all disillusioned by its negative results.

Heide understood, but resented, the need to report monthly to the police. He was registered as an alien. There is so much taken for granted in the benefits gained from living in the country of one's birth. He had lost his nationality, and his spirit and courage had begun to flag. The sadness of losing Paul to the Nazis towered above his other griefs. By the middle of 1939 he had given up all hope of contacting Paul. The need to occupy his spare time prompted Heide to work on voluntary committees that were engaged in helping the thousands of refugees flooding into Britain.

He created an association in London to bring together the Germans who had fled from Hitler. From this fraternity he gained many new friends. This, and his weekly visits to the Stevens, gradually gave him a new lease of life.

In May, Paula had given birth to a boy. The Stevens gave Heide the news over the phone. 'Paula is well, the birth was without any complications, but could you go and see her tomorrow? She is asking for you.'

The nursing home just south of Redhill was on a south-facing slope. The Weald stretched away to the distant Downs, and Paula's room looked onto this view.

'My dear Paula, you look so well,' he said, walking towards her bed and putting the flowers he had brought her on the bedside table.

He leaned down and kissed her on the forehead.

'Mr Heide, what gorgeous flowers! And thank you for coming so quickly.'

'And where's this beautiful baby I've heard about?'

'He'll be brought in soon.' She was propped up in bed. Heide could see that she was very close to tears.

'Please sit down,' she said.

For a short time neither spoke. Then they both said together, 'I've not heard from—' and they both laughed.

'I'm sorry, Paula, go on.'

The smile had disappeared from her face.

'I was going to say the same as you. As I told you before, I know that Paul was writing until the end of January; it was obvious from the way my father behaved each morning. He always took in the post from the postman. But since then I'm certain that he hasn't written a line.'

Heide said in a sad and resigned tone, 'I've had no news at all, Paula.'

'I sent him that one letter. I have never known if he received it.' She looked down at her hands which she had clasped together. Her sobbing started very quietly and slowly. It was a long moment before Heide realised she was crying.

He went over to her side, putting his arms around her shoulders, he said, 'If you want to have a good cry, do just that.' But her tears continued to come slowly. She gradually stopped, and to Heide she now looked tired and pale. 'Am I never going to see him again? I don't think I could bear that,' she said, her voice choked with emotion.

'Here's your handkerchief – now dry those tears away.' Heide returned to his chair and went on, 'I don't know, Paula. I've tried hard enough, God only knows, to find out where and how he is. I have found that by working hard and keeping my mind fully occupied, it helps me forget,' he was trying to get her away from thoughts of Paul. 'The important matter now is that you find a future for yourself.'

'He told me that he would call for me – that I would go to Germany. I want to do that more than anything else in the world.'

'Paula, that is the last place in the world for you to even visit, let alone live.' He hesitated and then said, 'I do not see how a war can be avoided. Should that happen, your country of birth is the one for you to be in – not a foreign one.'

'Mr Heide, what does that matter?' she replied with conviction. 'Look at you, Mr Heide.'

'My situation is different. I did not leave my country because I wanted to, but because I had to. If it was possible I'd go back tomorrow, but you, my dear, it's not the same, can't you see that?'

'All I know is that I love Paul. I have his baby. I've got to go to him. It's the one thing that's kept me going for the past nine months.' The tears welled in her eyes again. She said softly, 'If a war should start I would want to be with him. In a war people on both sides get killed. What matters then is to be with the ones you love.'

'That villain Hitler would not be to your liking, Paula.'

'I don't care about him! If the chance comes, I'll go to Paul.'

Please God let that not happen, thought Heide, and then the knock at the door announced the arrival of the baby.

Heide saw at once the likeness to Paul but he said, 'Now that is a beautiful child.' He peered at the baby, who gave him a windy smile. 'What are you going to call him?'

THE TRIUMPH OF LOVE AND LIBERTY

'If I called him Paul that would cause a blazing row at home, so for peace I'm calling him David John.' And then, as the nurse handed the child to her, she added, 'We can easily change the name later.'

As Heide rose later to leave she said, 'One of the nice things about being in this nursing home is the view from this window. I look over towards the South Downs and think, "Just over there is where Paul was at school".' She was looking in that direction as Heide closed the door.

Captain Ludecke, adjutant of Paul's training regiment, was giving his lecture on the history of the tank. This preceded his talk on the modern German armoured division.

'It is true to say that the English invented the tank, but they have not seen the possibilities of its use in future warfare. The nearest translation of the word *tank* in German in 1915 was *Schutzengrabenvernichtungpanzerkraftwagen*.' He got his usual laughs. 'Today that has been conveniently shorted to Panzer, and you can be proud of the fact that today also we lead the world in tank design and manoeuvrability. A fully equipped German armoured division is made up of: divisional headquarters, a divisional reconnaissance unit, an air force group of 46, dive bombers, two tank regiments, over four hundred tanks, a field artillery regiment...' The captain's harsh voice droned on and the heat of the lecture room made Paul feel drowsy. His thoughts turned to Paula. Their child would have been born in May. Had it been a boy or girl? He had often wondered.

How was Paula? He had stopped writing to her in the early part of the year, for he had realised that trying to get in touch with her was hopeless. He had taken Colonel Müller's advice to heart and become obsessed with his work. His progress in this had been impressive, and he had passed out top of his class in the wireless and gunnery sections.

Whenever he tried to speak to Richard about Paula his friend rapidly changed the subject, but in bed at night his thoughts soon turned to her. He had to find a way of making contact. One day in the middle of Ludecke's lecture he suddenly thought the best way of making contact would be through another Englishman – the British consul at Hanover. There was one there. He had passed the building on his visit to the city only last week during weekend leave. He would go there as soon as possible. How easily the problem had suddenly been solved.

He heard his name being called: 'Now, Heide, Heide,' repeated Ludecke in a loud voice, 'supposing you tell us all how many 20-mm guns there are in the anti-aircraft battalion of an armoured division.'

Paul came out of his dream and in a confident voice almost shouted the answer, 'Twenty, sir,' he guessed.

'You're only sixteen out – if you had been listening you would have known that there are thirty-six pieces of 20-mm guns. Have you been taking notes?'

The strictness of Ludecke was feared throughout the training regiments. Paul felt as though his stomach was on the edge of a cliff, soon to be dumped into space.

He said, 'No, sir – er, that is, I have taken some."

'Then,' replied Ludecke, 'you had better make sure that your roommate fills in any gaps. Failing your examination on this important lecture will result in downgrading to an earlier class.'

Later that night, as Paul copied the lecture notes he had missed from Richard's notebook, he told him of his idea of contacting the British consul at Hanover.

'Paul, isn't that girl out of your memory yet? What possible chance have you got of seeing her? Be realistic and forget her.'

'That's impossible – you see, I love her and that means not only will I never forget her, but also that I'm determined to get her out here, no matter how long it takes.'

'Suppose she doesn't want to come?'
'Don't be crazy, of course she does.'
Richard hardened his voice and replied, 'I wouldn't mind betting that your mind wandered to Paula during the lecture this afternoon. If you don't reconcile yourself to the inevitable, which means forgetting the girl, you are bound to find this softness of character frustrating your work, not only in the Army, but also for the Nazis. Remember your early training in the Youth Movement, remember the vows you took for Hitler, remember, in fact, all you have been taught in the past.'

Paul didn't reply, but continued his writing. He thought of his life at St Peter's. For the first time in his young life he faintly perceived the difference between democracy and dictatorship, but the picture was dim. He loved one individual, but he also loved a state, a country, a way of life. He was still blinded when he looked at the mirror of his mind.

St Peter's had taught Paul the virtue of courage, individual courage. It had unconsciously prepared him for life as a German. A dictatorship makes enormous demands on the courage of men, and he was certainly not lacking in courage!

Chapter Twenty-six

It was nearly the end of July before Paul could visit Hanover, and then only for a day. The officers' training course at Wolfenbüttel had been cut back by three months on direct orders from the Führer, who had completed his plans for the invasion of Poland by the end of June, supervising the final details at Berchtesgarden. The war he was planning would be total war, and he had demanded that the officer corps be enlarged as quickly as possible.

All leave had been indefinitely postponed but Paul's class had earned a day's respite by achieving high average marks in an examination.

Paul left the camp early, getting a lift to Brunswick in an Army truck. Within a short time he had hitchhiked a lift down the autobahn to Hanover.

The British consulate was in the Herrenhausen suburb of the city. The consul, Mr Hennessy-Jones, was an old Etonian.

When the consul's secretary told him there was a German soldier requesting an immediate interview he was perplexed.

'And why,' he asked, 'should a German soldier wish to see me?'

'Search me, sir,' relied the secretary, equally puzzled.

'Don't you think it might have been wiser to ask him what he wanted?' Then he asked, 'Can he speak English?' Hennessy-Jones' knowledge of German started with 'Ja' and ended with 'Nein'. 'Well, don't dither, old boy,' he continued, 'send him in and I'll jolly well soon find out.'

Paul entered the consul's office with the words, 'How do you do, sir, my name's Heide.'

Hennessy-Jones came round from his desk and his face broadened into a wide grin as he replied with relief, 'How do you do! I'm so glad you can speak English. Do sit down, old chap, and what can I do to help you?'

Where shall I start? thought Paul.

'Have a cigarette,' said Hennessy-Jones.

'Thanks.' The consul dropped the desk lighter while passing it to Paul and it landed on a glass ashtray and bounced off the desk onto Paul's foot. It was a large, heavy German-type lighter – and Paul's foot hurt.

'Dashed sorry, old boy,' Hennessy-Jones said. 'Are you all right? Frightfully clumsy of me.' His affected voice, though pleasing, was marred by its staccato and high-pitched tone.

Paul picked up the lighter. He wanted to rub his foot but said, 'Oh, I'm fine. It didn't hurt.' He lit his cigarette.

'Now, where were we? Yes – er – yes, what can I do to help you?'

'I was educated at St Peter's in England,' Paul started, 'and—'

'I say, old chap,' interrupted the consul, 'were you really? I had a cousin who went there. Frightfully "all upstairs", you know, brainy and that.' He stared at Paul. The German certainly spoke English without a trace of a foreign accent. But it was, he convinced himself, all a gigantic joke. Yes, he concluded, a new type of frivolity from England. *Right*, he thought, *I'll teach 'em. I'll play him along and pretend I believe.*

He said, 'Frightfully sorry to cut in, old boy – you were saying that you went to St Peter's. Do carry on.'

'There's not much else to add to that, but as I can only be here for today I'd like to get to the reason for my call as quickly as possible.'

'Do,' said Jones, as he leant back in his chair only pretending to listen. While Paul spoke, the consul spent most of the time thinking about a counter-joke to play against his staff. *How the blazes did the chap manage to get such an exact copy of the German uniform? Theatrical costumer, I suppose.*

Paul was encouraged by the consul's obvious interest in trying to help. He spoke for at least fifteen minutes before the older man posed a question.

'This girl of yours in London, and your uncle, how is it that they've been unable to contact you?' he asked.

'I told you, sir, her parents won't let her see any of my letters and they prevent her writing to me. I think it's best – don't you? – that under the circumstances I shouldn't make any contact with my uncle yet. Once I'm commissioned, then perhaps I should do something about that.'

'Dash it, old boy, yes, of course you must!' Hennessy-Jones said. 'Now look, I'm going to help you all I can – so would you like to leave everything to me for now?'

'Yes, of course, sir. I'm extremely grateful. I didn't imagine that it would be so easy, otherwise I would have come here months ago.'

You'll be back in here a damn sight sooner than you think, the consul thought with relish, but he said, 'Yes, but never you mind, the great thing is you've come at last, so off you go for now and I'll do all I can to help.'

Paul rose from his chair. Hennessy-Jones saw him to the door, where Paul repeated, 'I hope I'll have some good news soon, sir. You've got my address?'

'Yes, yes, of course I have, old chap. You'll hear from me soon.'

When Paul had gone, the consul returned to his desk and sat for some time staring at the notes he had taken: *The first secretary must be seen ... will not have this sort of thing going on ... a joke is a joke but ... dignity of my office...*

By the time Paul reached the autobahn at Hanover, Mr Hennessy-Jones had been convinced by his secretary that no joke had been played upon him.

'Oh Lord!' he said, and as he frantically looked through

his notes for a clue as to how to contact Paul, he muttered, 'I can't remember his name, his address, or much of his story. I recall certain scraps of information but nothing definite.'

'Oh, I say!' he then said out loud, 'I am a cad—' He turned to his secretary, 'Do you know, I rather liked the man and would have liked to help him.'

'Perhaps he'll come back, sir,' suggested the secretary.

'Yes – yes, perhaps he will. I hope so.' And he repeated, 'If only I could remember his name or where he came from.'

'He didn't give any details to me, sir.'

'No, well, never mind, he'll be back.'

When Paul got back to Wolfenbüttel in the late afternoon he went to his room. Richard wasn't there. Paul was glad. He didn't intend to tell anyone of his visit to the consul. With any luck he should hear from Paula within the next two or three weeks.

Chapter Twenty-seven

Four weeks after Paul's visit to the British consul at Hanover, England declared war against Germany. *And now*, thought Paul, *the chance of seeing Paula has gone.* He said as much to Richard.

'This is the best thing that could have happened from your point of view, Paul,' Richard answered. 'Germany is going to win this war – as our Führer has said, "There will never be another 11 November 1918 for this country." The war will probably be over very soon and then you will be with her again.'

'Maybe,' replied Paul. 'But I didn't think it would ever come to this.'

'Come to what?'

'To war, Richard. We were always told in the Youth Movement that the Führer's will would be done without the necessity for war. Don't you remember?'

'I only remember that we were taught that Hitler's rule must be obeyed. We were to be guided by his judgements. In any case, it's Britain who has declared war on us.'

'Yes, you're right. It's just that for me at this moment I cannot make myself believe that war has begun with England.'

'The sooner you do that the better. I told you before that we would win any future war. Paul, I'm going to sleep.'

Paul sat on the edge of his bed. Why had he heard nothing from Paula? The consul had promised that he would make contact with her within a week or so.

Thinking of her filled him with desire – but was that all she really meant to him? He had read somewhere that women did remain faithful when they were in love, but that it was different for men. But he had made no effort to meet another girl, and there were plenty of them in Wolfenbüttel. He couldn't go with another girl; he would wait for her, and he was sure that she would wait for him.

Earlier in the day he had read the personal message from the Führer which had been sent to all Army establishments. It took him some minutes to push through the crowd of excited cadets to read the message. Hitler had stressed how much he had wanted peace, but the West had firmly rejected his moves in this direction. He knew that the German Army was behind him to a man, and even at this late hour he hoped for peace. One thing was certain, the message had continued, 'in wars there had never been two victors, but very often only losers. Let those who consider war to be the better solution reject my outstretched hand.' Thus did the leader neatly sidestep his responsibility for the outbreak of hostilities.

The young Nazis in the camp received the news with joy, and Paul had been swept away with the emotion. In Wolfenbüttel, as in many German towns, stunned crowds had listened to the radio announcements blaring out on the public address systems. They found it difficult to believe that Hitler had led them into a world of war.

Colonel Müller said to his adjutant, 'God help Germany if we lose the war.'

As Paul got into bed he reckoned that the war would indeed soon be over, but he was not very clear as to how it would end, and even less certain when he would get Paula over to Germany now. He couldn't know that within six months the glories of fighting for the Third Reich would bring him so much credit, and although Paula would never be far from his thoughts, the tide of events was destined to keep her very much at the back of his mind.

* * *

Erik Heide had been ordered to report to the Foreign Office within twelve hours after Chamberlain's declaration of war.

There were two men both sitting behind a large desk. The heavily built man asked Heide to sit down. The other was glancing through some papers. It was this man who spoke next.

'Mr Heide, you won't know us – I must confess we knew little of you until reading this file.' The man speaking was small, his bald head covered by one long thick strand of hair which was combed forward from the back of his head. He reminded Heide of Napoleon.

'But,' the man continued, 'in view of this war, all foreign nationals are of course being roped in. There are some exceptions – some to be interviewed before they are detained under the emergency regulations.'

Heide had expected this and said, 'Naturally, gentlemen, I understand.'

'You have already done some work for this country,' continued the second man. He paused and then said, 'What is your position now?'

'In regard to my loyalties?' asked Heide.

'Yes.'

'I am German,' he said, 'but I hate Hitler! He is an evil fascist. He is destroying my country.' He paused. 'England respects the individual. I have always believed in the individual.' He paused again.

'Do you think you'll win this war?' he asked.

'Of course, Mr Heide.'

'Why?'

'Because right is on our side.'

'And does right always win?' asked Heide.

'In the long run, yes.'

Heide admired the man's confidence.

'I pray to God you're right,' he said. 'I want to see the Nazis defeated, but in the process many good Germans will die.'

'Many good allies will no doubt die as well.'

'And then what happens?'

The heavily built man answered, saying, 'This time, Mr Heide, no doubt Germany will be crushed once again.'

'I hope I live long enough to return to Germany if Hitler loses this war – though I'm not certain about that. Germany must find the right men to lead her.'

'You will, I know, forgive me when I quote the saying, "The German is either at your feet or at your throat".'

'Wellington was very pleased to see one at Waterloo,' Heide said quietly.

'We've wandered in our conversation,' cut in the smaller man. 'Are we correct in assuming that your attitude is of not wanting either to help or to hinder?'

'That's a good way of putting it, gentlemen – at any rate for the moment. My age prevents any active participation, but perhaps in some way I can be of small assistance. Translating and interpreting German, for instance.'

'You realise that you will be detained in prison for a while? It's better from your point of view that nothing is known of your previous espionage work. It has been decided on higher authority that this is the course to take.'

'Naturally. I'm also grateful that what I did for your country is to remain a secret. I never considered for one moment that I was spying against Germany. It was against Hitler and the Nazis.'

'Have you had news of your nephew in Germany?'

'No, have you?' Heide asked hopefully.

'Nothing at all. Strange case, especially after an education at St Peter's.'

'The Nazis got him at an earlier age,' replied Heide. 'It shows how easily boys' minds can be poisoned, even English ones!'

Before Heide was taken to Wormwood Scrubs, where he was to remain for six months, he phoned Paula.

'Prison! But that's absurd, Mr Heide!' she had cried.

'No, it's not – it's quite normal practice in time of war. It is very likely that I'll be released after a short stay.'

'But what about your business?'

'Ah, that's another matter. The agency has gone into voluntary liquidation. There is plenty of money for me.'

'Can I come and visit you?'

'I hope so! Yes, of course you can.' Then he added, 'How's David?'

'He's fine. I'm going to wait for Paul, you know.'

'You are, my dear? I'm glad of that.'

Chapter Twenty-eight

Paul and Richard were commissioned to the same tank regiment a fortnight before the first Christmas of the war. Within a month Colonel Müller was posted as its commanding officer. The regiment, the Sixth Panzer, was equipped with the Panzer IV tank. Once Müller had settled in, he commenced a rigorous tactical training programme.

Müller had held a conference with the officers at his headquarters in Münster. He told them of his plans to make the regiment the best in the German Army. He could promise them only hard work, and now that every member of the regiment had enjoyed a spell of leave, no more would be granted for at least six months.

At the end of his talk he lifted his hand slightly in a careless 'Heil Hitler' salute. Later that day Paul was ordered to report to his office.

'Sit down, Lieutenant Heide. Have you got used to your rank yet?' he smiled.

'More or less, sir. It's a great thrill being saluted by the men.'

'Yes, but always remember that it is given to you as a sign of respect, not only to you personally, but also to the Army. Treat it as an outward acknowledgement of everything we stand for. That was instilled in you at Wolfenbüttel.'

'Yes, sir. Walldern and myself are glad that you are in command.'

'I shouldn't be too sure of that,' smiled Müller, and he went on, 'I have had a letter from Herr Seebohm.'

'Yes, sir. How is he?'

'I have no idea. But he is now in a high position in Berlin – political, of course.' Müller stopped for a moment and looked at Paul. 'You may smoke if you wish.'

Paul lit a cigarette as Müller continued, 'He has asked me to send a report on you to Berlin.'

'What sort of report, sir?'

'Just a general one. I detect, though, that he thinks you are wasted in the Army.'

Paul inhaled deeply and the smoke drifted out of his nose as he replied, 'What does he mean, wasted'?'

'It probably relates to your English education – he thinks that that can be put to good use.' Müller waited a long while and then said, 'They might want to send you to England to spy.'

Paul lent across and stubbed his cigarette out on an ashtray, sat back in his chair, and said, 'That would be too chancy, sir. I could easily be recognised.'

'But supposing, Heide, you went back and convinced them that you had given up the Nazi cause and then went on working for Germany?'

Paul smiled and said, 'What with Colonel Bedford and then me, St Peter's will be getting quite a name for espionage. Do you remember his case, sir?'

'I do, very well. So he was at the same school?'

'Not only that, he virtually got me into it.'

Müller looked surprised, but these things did not interest him. 'What are your views, Heide?'

'I will do whatever the Party considers is of most use to it. But,' he continued, 'I would much prefer to stay in this regiment – we've been told the war will soon be over and—'

'Soon be over!' cried Müller. 'It hasn't even started yet! I very much doubt whether it will be over soon.' He started to read Seebohm's letter again.

'Heide, I have got to reply to this letter. Depending on

what you say, your immediate future will be decided on. Can I take it that you want to stay with this regiment?'

'Yes, sir, very much.'

'I'll see what I can do. In fact, you can be certain that you will stay with us. That's all for now, you may go.'

Paul no longer made the mistake of giving the Nazi salute in front of the colonel, but he had noticed that he himself had given an indifferent one at the conference – probably for the benefit of his squadron leaders who were ardent supporters of Hitler. As he reached the door, Müller said, 'Have you heard from your foster uncle?'

'No, sir, nor from my girl in England.'

'I'm sorry to hear that – you will one day.'

As Paul walked back to his quarters he suddenly realised how much he liked Müller. He had respected him at Wolfenbüttel, but now this had developed into a higher esteem, bordering on hero worship.

Although leave had been stopped, the officers and men of the Sixth Panzer were able to enjoy their evenings in Münster. One evening late in February 1940 Richard took Paul to a club on the outskirts of the city. The barmaid was kept busy but, although young, she was too skinny, pale and ugly to be anything but safe from any advances by the young German soldiers. They took their drinks to one of the small tables which surrounded the tiny dance floor.

'You've got Paula out of your system now, haven't you Paul?' said Richard.

'No, I haven't – and please don't mention her – it's difficult enough for me as it is.' Paul looked angry.

'All right, Paul, don't get agitated. It's just that as you have come out with me tonight and it's the first time you've done that, I thought perhaps...'

'Well, I haven't, so just drop it, will you?'

Paul saw the two girls approach their table. 'Come on, Richard,' he said, 'this is a terrible place. Drink up and let's get out of here.'

Richard was inclined to agree and then, as he lifted his glass to his mouth, he saw the two girls too.

'Look, Paul, aren't they something?'

The girl who sat next to Paul was wearing a black silk dress so closely cut that it fitted like a glove.

'What's your name?' she said. 'Mine's Daniela.'

'Paul,' and then, 'would you like a drink?'

As she turned to speak to her friend, Paul noticed the slide fastener up the spine of her dress. He found himself staring at her back.

'You're the first girl I've spoken to for ages.'

'Why, that's wonderful! I'm very surprised to hear that. You're very good looking.' Richard had taken his girl onto the dance floor.

'Are we going to dance?' she asked him.

'You can if you want,' he said.'

'You have appalling manners.'

'I'm sorry, that was rude. Yes, come on, let's have a dance.'

On the floor she held herself very close to him.

'Do you like dancing?' Daniela whispered in his ear.

'Not very much.'

'I love it! I love it!'

'Do you? Then you can't be enjoying this very much.'

'Oh, but I am!'

They returned to the table and then the drink started to flow. Richard said to Paul later, 'I'm off now – see you in the morning.' Paul wanted to go but he remained seated as Richard left with his girl.

With each dance and each drink Paul felt his resistance weaken. Around midnight he started playing with her zip fastener. 'This is fun,' he said.

'It's more fun for me than it is for you,' she lied. Her head was on his shoulder and then, moving her lips against his chin, she mumbled, 'What time is it?'

'Around midnight.'

'Shall we go back to my place?'

'Yes.'

The moment they walked into her living room she fell swiftly into his arms. He began to kiss her.

'We mustn't waste time,' she said. He enjoyed the feeling of lust. He ran his fingers through her hair and kissed her as hard and in as many places as he could reach.

'Wait in here a moment.'

A few minutes later she called to him from her bedroom. 'Come on, Paul.' As he entered the room he saw her lying motionless on the bed. He swiftly undressed and as quickly lay down beside her.

'Oh,' she moaned professionally.

He said, 'I just want to hold you in my arms quietly for a little while.'

'You're a funny boy.'

He kissed her forehead, her eyes, her cheeks, her throat, her mouth, but without passion. She did the same to him, but with greater fervour. 'Come along,' she pleaded, 'be a nice boy.'

Later, when he put out his right hand and switched on the light, he pushed it away to keep the beam from her eyes. His watch showed four o'clock. He got out of bed without disturbing her, dressed and left some money on her bedside table.

It was when he got into his room at the barracks that he felt a wave of disgust about the whole evening. Then he realised for the first time that Paula had not entered his mind once. He felt dirty and ashamed. He was still awake when his batman called him.

He met Richard at breakfast. 'How did you get on, Paul? My girl was as hot as a stove.'

Paul said nothing in reply, but wondered if Paula still loved him or whether she had found someone else.

Paul's troop of tanks consisted of four Panzer IVs. His squadron commander, Major Friedrich Hossbach, controlled five such troops.

A corporal in turn commanded each tank. During Colonel Müller's intensive training programme, Paul went to great lengths to gain the confidence of his own crew, as well as of his corporal. His efficiency and personality soon gained their respect. This was difficult and important for a tank officer as there is always close and personal contact with the men.

He gained favour with them by always insisting on a high standard of turnout, and from this he achieved discipline and strict, rapid obedience to his orders.

His corporals soon realised that he had studied beforehand exactly what he intended to do and the lessons he intended to teach. At the same time, Paul treated them as rational human beings and was scrupulously fair and just in all his dealings with them.

By April 1940 Paul had worked his troop into an effective fighting force. Colonel Müller had done likewise with the regiment. The main problem now for the officers of the Sixth Panzer regiment was how to maintain this momentum and prevent boredom. Action seemed as far away as ever.

During this period, Colonel Müller suggested to Paul that he should give a lecture to the regiment on England. The colonel said to him, 'To know your enemy is to know his faults and failings. This could be of great use.'

'What exactly do you want me to say, sir?' Paul asked him.

'I will leave that to you – but would you like to make an attempt?'

'Yes, sir, I'll try.'

Paul was given a week in which to prepare his talk. When he told Richard, his friend suggested that he tell the regiment about Paula.

'I think I'll tell them about you,' retorted Paul, and followed this with a well-aimed throw of a shoe which just missed Richard, who rapidly retreated through the door.

As Paul prepared his talk, his mind began to fill with thoughts of the years he had spent in England. As he made the comparisons between the Nazis and the way of life in Britain, he became even more convinced that his choice of Germany was the right one. It seemed to him that the apathetic approach to youth and its problems in England virtually guaranteed the country's gradual decline. Compared with Hitler's Germany, England in the 1930s was hopelessly out of date.

This gave Paul the foundation of his talk, throughout which he constantly laid stress on the two countries' approach to youth. His talk went well but he was unprepared for the questions which came at the end. Colonel Müller rose to congratulate Paul and to thank him for his interesting lecture. Lieutenant Heide, he thought to himself, had given a perfect propaganda report on the benefits gained by being a young Nazi. Would the world, he pondered, ever have the chance to find out how deeply Hitler was despised by thousands of Germans?

The colonel had announced that Heide would be prepared to answer any questions from any member of the regiment. He then sat down and Paul's squadron leader, Major Hossbach, rose.

'Lieutenant Heide has been in the unique position of choosing between our system and that of England. Could he now confirm that as England is decadent, its fall will be rapid and conquest by the Third Reich easy?'

Paul answered, 'I am still a young man and therefore do not have any means of answering that question fully, sir, but from what our Führer tells us, there is every likelihood that England may come to terms with Germany even now. Should this not happen, then I would say from my experience in England that our glorious armies would be able to sweep through the country rapidly.'

Colonel Müller got up and added that first we would have to get to England, and second, many months or even years of hard fighting might then follow, but he wanted to ask Lieutenant Heide what in his experience the English thought of the Germans.

Paul said, 'With the greatest of respect, sir, not very much.' He then went on, 'There were numerous occasions, both at my school and outside, when Germany was not only spoken of with bitter disrespect, but also in terms of hatred.'

Müller asked him to give examples of this hatred and for the first time he was lost for words. For a very long moment he hesitated, then he started to mumble about his house master at school and a taxi driver in London... He eventually saved himself acute embarrassment by quoting long tracts of anti-British propaganda he had recently learnt from Nazi pamphlets.

Thereafter the questions were answered curtly and indifferently by Paul; he seemed to lose his confidence.

Müller called him aside after the talk.

'You'll be pleased to hear that you are to stay with the regiment, at any rate for the time being.'

'Thank you very much, sir,' he replied, and then, 'You know, sir, there is a very strong anti-German feeling in England. When you asked for examples it wasn't easy without preparation to think of many, but it's there all right, and very strong.'

Müller had hoped that Paul would have said something different – that there was a feeling of regard in England for Germany, at least while Paul had been living there – but he said. 'I'm sure you are correct. As I said to the regiment just now, the main problem is for us to defeat them.'

But as Paul walked away, Müller reflected on how tragic it was that for the second time in his life the countries of Europe were at each other's throats. Only this time the Fatherland was commanded by a corporal-turned-dictator.

Chapter Twenty-nine

The Sixth Panzer regiment moved towards the Western front from Münster on a fine spring day at the end of the first week of May. The 'Sitzkrieg' as the Germans called the lull in fighting since the declaration of war, or the 'phoney war' as the British called it, was over.

Within a few days Hitler issued his order of the day to the German Army.

> *Soldiers of the Western Front! Now your hour has come. The struggle which begins today will determine the fate of the German nation for the next thousand years. Now do your duty! The entire German people are with you and wish you well!*

It was signed and dated: *Berlin, May 10, 1940, Adolf Hitler*

Shortly after dawn on 14 May the Sixth Panzer regiment crashed through the French lines near Sedan. Within ten days the regiment was in sight of Dunkirk. Then the division to which the regiment belonged was halted on direct orders from Hitler. Colonel Müller was called by his divisional commander, General Rommel – it was 24 May.

'Why on earth have we halted?' Müller asked the general and then continued, 'We have suffered very few casualties – we can be in Dunkirk within hours.'

'The orders are direct from the Führer, Colonel Müller,' said the general. 'They are to be obeyed, though I confess I am puzzled. We must wait.'

Two days passed before the order to advance was given,

but this belated order enabled the cornered British Army to strengthen its defences and escape to the sea that lay behind.

The stubborn British and French defence of Dunkirk's perimeter was for many days unbreakable. Paul's squadron, which had advanced hundreds of miles in a matter of days, now found that to gain a hundred yards became costly in men and tanks. His squadron commander, Major Hossbach, ordered his troop leaders to his headquarters for a briefing.

'The British are trying to escape by sea. It is vital that we capture Dunkirk and prevent this happening. Lieutenants Heide and Walldern – your two troops will this afternoon give tactical support to 316 regiment who are to attack the town from the south. The other troops will remain here in reserve. The two of you will report immediately to the commanding officer of that regiment.'

As they left Paul turned to Richard. 'I don't like the idea of this very much.'

'What's wrong?' enquired Richard.

'We're going to be sitting targets.'

'Maybe – but the war's almost won.'

Later, after meeting the infantry commander, Paul felt happier. 'At least we're having the dive bombers go in first to soften them up.'

'Don't worry, Paul, we will waltz through them.'

'We tried that three days ago,' Paul smiled, referring to their evening with the two women. 'But I wish you wouldn't liken this to dancing.'

'Why not? We will soon be in Paris – there'll be plenty of dancing there.'

'Am advancing with infantry now,' reported Paul over his wireless.

'Good luck,' replied Hossbach, and then, as if for encouragement, 'See you in Dunkirk.'

As the Germans advanced, the defenders of Dunkirk opened their guns on them and the losses were heavy. Paul's tanks had positioned themselves behind the first line of infantry, and he could see Richard's in a similar position half a mile away on his left flank.

The men surrounding Paul's troop of tanks suddenly disappeared as they were either killed or wounded or took cover. The enemy was firm and unyielding. Their fire was coming from cleverly concealed nests among the wooded slopes dominating the main road into the town.

Through his binoculars Paul could see some of the enemy soldiers quite plainly one moment, and the next they would vanish. He thought, *They're not throwing much at us.* He reported on the wireless, 'Infantry round us suffering badly but no anti-tank fire.'

'In that case go for them,' replied Hossbach.

Over the wireless Paul heard one of Richard's corporals report that his troop commander's tank had been hit and was out of action.

Paul heard this as if in the distance as he gave orders to his corporals to fire on the wooded slopes. To his own gunner, he ordered, 'Seventy-five millimetres, traverse left, steady, steady, on target – range five hundred, enemy in slopes of wood. Can you see them, gunner?'

'No, sir.'

'Doesn't matter. In that general direction, fire!'

Paul's tanks aimed their shells at the trees, hoping that they would burst over and down on the enemies' heads. Where the dive bombers had failed to make an impression, the accurate tank fire succeeded, and another line of infantry appeared around Paul's tank and the company commander climbed onto his tank.

'That seems to have quietened them down. Shall we have another go?'

'All right by me, sir,' said Paul.

No sooner did the advance continue than a withering fire recommenced from the allied lines. Again the Germans were forced to ground.

The company commander returned to Paul. 'Can't you rush them and ferret them out?'

'Not without losing all my tanks, sir. How can I be sure there are no anti-tank guns?'

'You'll find that out by advancing. I am the senior officer, I command you to advance.'

'I don't act on your orders.'

Paul gave Major Hossbach a situation report on the air. 'You must make your own decision,' he replied.

Paul ordered his tanks to cross the open field in which they were positioned and make for the main road. He felt too vulnerable in the middle of the flat open space.

To the company commander he said, 'I'm going to make for the main road and drive straight up it. If I get there, will you advance rapidly to support us?'

'Yes,' was the only reply. As Paul made for the road with his other tanks following in line, he heard over the wireless that Richard had been killed. A shiver ran down his back and he felt very frightened, but in his mind he burned to avenge Richard's death.

For a short moment he thought of the peculiar situation he was in. Over there one thousand yards or so away, men were trying to get back to England. Were any St Peter's boys among them? Until nine months ago he never thought he would be fighting England, but now, in the heat of battle, the sense of self-preservation and the need to look after his men built inside him a hatred for these men in the woods.

He was leading his tanks and reached the road first. As he did so, all hell was let loose. Guns from the Allied position were targeted at them very quickly. He ordered his driver to reverse back into the comparative shelter of a ditch and signalled the other tanks to do the same. Then he looked up the main road to Dunkirk.

The confusion was indescribable. The road was littered

with smashed cars and horses that had died in harness. The stench of their rotting carcasses filled his nostrils. There were also many bomb craters. He quickly saw that it would be impossible to go up that road.

He reported as much to Hossbach. 'You had better make contact with the infantry again,' he was ordered.

As Paul returned he saw the infantry frantically digging in. He passed a lieutenant who was pulling a bullet out of a corporal's cheekbone with a pair of pliers. German dead were everywhere and stretcher bearers were running and stumbling in their efforts to save the wounded. Paul saw two of them disintegrate from the burst of a shell which landed only a few yards away.

He jumped down from his tank when he saw the infantry commander sheltering in a quickly dug trench. He wished he hadn't left his tank – although it was an open target, he felt much safer inside it.

'It's quite impossible to get up the main road. It's completely blocked by vehicles,' Paul shouted above the uproar.

'These guns that fired at you on the road – they're coming from three British tanks. Look over there!'

Paul saw them through his binoculars. They were in good positions on either side of the road, just short of the woods.

'I think they've been dug in – they are so low down.'

At that moment a messenger arrived from the rear with the order that the infantry was to advance no matter how costly it was in lives.

'Well, this looks like it,' said the company commander.

'I'll advance with you and do the best I can to help,' Paul replied.

On returning to his tank, his wireless operator told him that he was wanted on the air. It was Müller. 'The rest of your squadron, plus another one, is on the way to help you. Do not move until they arrive.'

'The infantry is about to attack. I have said I'll go with them.'

'That's very brave of you, but I am not going to lose tanks unnecessarily. You will remain where you are until the others arrive.'

'But they are advancing now. I must go with them!'

'Stay where you are!' was the firm order given in reply.

Paul saw the infantry soldiers running forward, making as much use as possible of any available cover. He could see that the attack was sure to fail. His tanks did their best to give covering fire but soon had to stop because of the danger of hitting their own troops, who suddenly started to veer across the line of fire.

He reported this over the air. This time Hossbach replied, 'Can you see the other tanks yet?' Paul could see the dust they were raising about a mile away.

'Yes, but by the time they get here I don't think they'll be of much use.'

Müller cut in on the air, 'You can advance to contact the infantry.'

Paul gave his order quickly to his tanks.

'All tanks to advance to line abreast!' he shouted into his microphone.

The German infantry was being forced back as Paul and his troop advanced through its broken lines.

Paul saw the gun that registered direct hits on two of his tanks. The British tanks' guns could not penetrate the armour of the Panzer IV tanks, but this one did – a cunningly hidden anti-aircraft gun aiming horizontally.

He gave brief and curt firing orders to his gunner: 'Seventy-five millimetres, traverse right, steady, steady, steady, on four hundred gun at base of tree, camouflaged.'

'On target,' his gunner shouted.

'Fire.'

Three rounds later the gun had been silenced. Paul had

seen two of his men bale out of one of his hit tanks. He turned his tank round and set off to pick them up.

Hossbach came over the air, 'Pull back, pull back! Attack called off.'

Both of the hit tanks were ablaze, the ammunition inside exploding. He could see no sign of his men and, signalling to his other tanks to follow, turned towards his own lines.

Müller saw Paul on his return to headquarters.

'You did well, Heide,' he said, 'but no doubt you have learned a lot about fighting from this. You see those British can fight hard when the spirit moves them.' He paused. 'All the crew of one of your tanks were killed. Two escaped from the other. They were lucky to do so, for they were shot at while trying to get out of the tank.' He looked at Paul and continued. 'What's an English phrase that would sum that up, Heide?'

'They would say that that's not cricket.' His dirty and dust-covered face broke into a small grin, which quickly vanished as he went on, 'It seems only a few minutes ago that Lieutenant Walldern was saying that the war would soon be over, and now he's dead.' To Paul, Richard had funny ways and many faults, but they had had a close friendship since meeting at Wolfenbüttel.

'You know his parents, Heide. I will be writing to them. I suggest you do the same.'

'Yes, I will, sir,' replied Paul.

Dunkirk, defended stubbornly by the British and French, held out until the morning of 4 June. As the Sixth Panzer regiment entered the town, the remaining defenders laid down their arms. Paul had quickly received two reinforcement tanks and crews and it was his troop which was the first to enter the

Place Jean Bart, the principal square in the town. White flags of surrender could be seen everywhere, small white splashes of cloth sticking out of the remains of shop fronts, larger ones tied to the remnants of buildings surrounding the square. It was also in this square that a large number of the British had assembled. Most of the battle-weary men were sitting down. Colonel Müller had given instructions that the prisoners of war were to be directed towards the rear German lines and Paul had already waved to hundreds of them on entering the town, indicating the way they should go. The first ones had been French, and now he was seeing the first of the British.

His tanks had taken positions which dominated the square and, giving orders that he was to be covered by their guns, he dismounted from his tank and approached the British.

Two of the officers walked towards him, one of them holding a bayonet with a handkerchief tied to its blade. This man was a few paces behind the other, who, at a pace or so from Paul, stopped and saluted.

This man, a colonel whose salute was returned by Paul, announced in shaky German, 'I am Colonel Waite, of the Royal Sussex regiment. My battalion has been ordered to surrender.'

To the Englishman's surprise, Paul answered, 'Yes, Colonel, as you hear I speak English.' He paused and then said, 'My orders are that any prisoners of war are to find their way to the southern outskirts of the town, where further instructions will await them.'

And then, at the same moment, over the colonel's shoulder, Paul recognised the junior officer standing a few paces behind.

Chapter Thirty

'Bright!' he shouted, 'John Bright!' Paul would have remembered that turned-up nose anywhere.

'Good Lord, it's Heide. Paul Heide!' returned Bright.

'You know this German, Bright?' said the colonel with even more astonishment.

'Know him, sir? I'll say I do. We were at school together.'

Paul went across to him and they shook hands, but neither said anything. They just stood there, looking at each other.

Some of the soldiers had stood up and watched with surprise as Paul and John started laughing at each other in the middle of the shattered square.

'Are you all right?' Paul asked solicitously.

'Terrible,' John answered. 'Even worse now, seeing you.'

It was then that they both laughed out loud together.

'What are you doing here, John?'

'Fighting.' And then, 'Were you in any of those tanks that tried to break through from the south a few days back?'

'Was I! I'll say I was – and you weren't by any chance on those wooded slopes throwing I don't know how much muck at us?'

'Where else?' laughed John. He continued, 'You caused quite a stir when you left England. I knew that you would one day go and live in Germany. I didn't think that we'd ever meet up again like this, though.'

They started to talk of St Peter's and recalled many memories of the place as the tired and weary Colonel Waite wandered back towards a group of officers.

'I saw your uncle in London, just after the New Year.'

'How was he?'

'He seemed well – he was interned at the outbreak, but only for a few months. You know about Paula, of course.'

'Of course not – what news have you?'

'Didn't you hear anything?'

'Nothing at all.' Paul, the victor, looked down at his shoes and said, 'She was going to have a baby – I was hoping to get her to Germany. Then he looked at John anxiously. 'What news have you got about her?'

'Not very much, except that your uncle said she was well and had gone to live somewhere in the country with her mother, her father and—'

'But have you any news about the baby?' cut in Paul.

'The baby was fine – did you know it was a boy?'

Thank God she's well, thought Paul. He said, 'No, John, I didn't know.'

Paul's wireless operator came up and reported that he was wanted on the air. 'Wait here, John.'

It was Hossbach, wanting a report.

'Nothing unusual to report. Large numbers of prisoners should be on their way back towards you by now.'

'Yes,' said Hossbach, 'they're coming past us all the time. No opposition, is there?'

'No,' replied Paul. 'I have just made contact with many British. They'll be coming your way soon.'

Paul jumped down from his tank again. The British were now forming a sort of order among themselves. They were being lined up three and four deep across the end of the square.

John had stayed in the same place.

As Paul went up to him he said, 'Do you hate me very much, John?'

'No, why should I? I wouldn't have spoken to you if I did. I used to think that you were crazy to rush off to Germany. Now all this has happened, I'm not so sure. It looks as if Germany has won this war.'

'There's still a large French Army to beat in the south,' said Paul. 'But you are right, we have won, or will do very soon.' Paul wanted more news of Paula. He continued, 'Have you any other news of Paula?'

'No more than I've given you. Had you really heard nothing?'

'Nothing.'

'There's no more I can tell you, except that your uncle was very concerned about you. He likes you a lot, you know, Paul.'

'Do you know how Paula feels about me?'

'I got the impression from your uncle that she is still very fond of you. Your uncle didn't seem happy about that – from her point of view, you understand.'

'Yes, yes – thank you, John – thank you, John.'

John smiled thinly and said, 'Our colonel has just been saying that we will all be back in England in a few months. He cannot see how any position can be raised against you.'

'He's dead right – I don't know what's going to happen next, but I feel the Führer will be able to bring about many improvements in England.'

'I don't know what you mean by that, Paul. I certainly can't see anything stopping you now, but I pray to God we don't have the sort of bloody dictatorship you've got.'

Paul's manner started to change. 'Don't talk like that, John. Hitler is good – he has been for Germany and he's just about to do the same for Europe,' he said curtly.

'Paul, I've always liked you but I've heard enough about the goings-on in Germany to say that it won't be much use trying that in England.'

'Not so fast, John, be careful what you say. I'm German now and I'm proud of being a Nazi.'

'The hell you are – I don't think you know what it's all about!'

The strain of the past months' campaign began to overcome the young men's feelings. 'I don't think, John, that you are in any position to express an opinion as to what I know and don't know. It may interest you to know, however, that whereas you are on your way to a prisoners' camp, I shall remain free and continue to fight, if necessary, for Germany.'

'Oh, why don't you keep your trap shut!' shouted John, losing patience. 'You know what I really think of you? You're a lousy turncoat bastard, and that's probably what everyone in England who knew you thinks, too.' And then, after a pause, he added, 'Paula as well.'

'You've no proof of that!' Paul was frightened by the possible truth of John's remarks. 'As a matter of fact, I was going to see if there was any way in which I could help you. But now you can climb up the bloody wall!'

'That's exactly what I intend to do if I'm put in a camp!' Then realising that Paul seemed put out by his previous remarks, he said, 'It's true what I said – there is a saying, Paul, that men run away to other countries because they are no good in their own.'

'I did not happen to run away,' cut in Paul, 'I had no need to – for Germany was home to me.' And then he turned his back on John and walked quickly towards his tanks.

It was about an hour later that the British started to march out of the square. Paul's tanks had maintained the same positions. Paul was sitting on the turret of his tank as the British soldiers marched past. John Bright was at the head of the column leading his platoon. As he drew level with Paul he looked towards him and smiled. 'Sorry about that shouting match – the worst is over now for all of us – I hope,' he said.

'Good luck, John,' Paul shouted back. 'I'm sorry, too. Take care of yourself, and Floreat St Peter's!'

'Floreat Peace,' returned John.

Paul replied, 'Floreat and Heil Hitler.'

* * *

Three months later, Paula got news of this meeting from Heide. John had written to his parents and asked them to pass the information about Paul on to Heide.

Chapter Thirty-one

After the fall of France, Paul's regiment returned to Germany for a rest and refit period. Leave was also granted, and as Paul had received a standing invitation to visit Richard's parents at Bad Harzburg, he wrote to them and accepted their offer. They had appreciated his letter to them on the death of their son, and in spite of Paul's obvious support for the Nazis, they were eager to hear of the manner of Richard's death. As with many parents of men killed on active service, they would never know complete peace of mind again, but so many had their sufferings eased by an account of how their sons had died. So often the whole truth was never told, but that didn't matter. As long as they could talk to someone who had been near the scene, the feeling of grief was shared, and this invariably helped.

And so it was for the Wallderns. After dinner on Paul's first evening of his stay, the doctor and his wife settled Paul into the most comfortable deckchair in the garden. It was a beautiful evening – the distant Harz mountains were echoing the sound of cattle bells across the valley, the setting sun silhouetted the mountain tops, the grass was green and lush, and the peace of Bad Harzburg made the war seem a lifetime away.

'It's so peaceful here,' said Paul. 'I wish I could stay here for ever.' He started to think of Paula and what she might be doing at this moment in time. For a while no one spoke, then Frau Walldern broke the silence.

'How did Richard die, Paul?' she asked.

The moment Paul had dreaded had come. He remembered

looking into the turret of Richard's tank. All that remained of his friend had been the top half of his body. The lower part had been severed by the shell that had penetrated the front of his tank and finished its flight in Richard's stomach.

Paul replied, 'I didn't see the hit which knocked out his tank – I went along afterwards. It would have been over very quickly, and neither Richard nor his crew could have known what hit them.' He paused and looked at the doctor, and addressing his remarks to him, said, 'All his crew were killed. It was so pointless, for the battle was nearly over. I think I told you in my letter that he was given a military funeral and buried in the churchyard of a village a few miles south of Dunkirk.' Paul stopped, hoping that was all they would want to know.

The doctor filled and lit his pipe. Frau Walldern wanted to find out more.

'How was it that the enemy were able to do this? We read in the papers that there was virtually no opposition.'

'I'm sorry, Frau Walldern,' Paul replied. *What else is there to say?* he thought, but he went on. 'There were many places where there was little or no resistance. It just happened that at Dunkirk a massive defence was arranged to prevent us breaking through to the beaches from which the British were evacuating.'

Doctor Walldern was now puffing clouds of smoke into the still evening air. He said in a slow voice and one full of emotion, 'We understand, Paul. It must have been very unpleasant at times. We can't help feeling, though – and it is almost as depressing as Richard's death – that he has perhaps died in vain.'

'Surely not,' said Paul. 'It is of course terrible that Richard has been killed, but to say it was in vain is wrong, so very wrong. The Third Reich is about to conquer Europe, perhaps the whole world. The Führer had warned us that sacrifices would be necessary, and—'

'Richard was our whole world, Paul,' interrupted Doctor Walldern. 'You know, Paul,' he continued, 'there are many Germans who do believe that Germany mustn't win this war, because they do not want to see the power of Hitler spread further.'

'Those are dangerous words to use, Herr Doctor. You could be reported for saying things like that.'

'And then?'

'And then you would be arrested.'

'That proves my point! I believe in freedom of speech – that's just one thing we do not enjoy now.'

'There's a war on,' Paul said. 'Such talk would be considered treason in any country.'

'Quite so, Paul, but you should also remember that it also applied before this country was at war.'

Frau Walldern's expression was worried. She looked quickly from her husband and back to Paul and said, 'I don't think we should talk about that any more.'

'My dear,' said her husband, 'of course we should. It's all part of what we feel about Richard.' And then, turning to Paul, he continued, 'In this country there is a contrast between private feelings and public action. Do you seriously imagine that all Germans are behind Hitler?'

'Herr Doctor,' said Paul, 'I was a good friend of Richard's and I understand your feelings after what has happened, but I would ask you to remember that I am also a Nazi and a great believer in the rightness and justness of our case. I must ask you to refrain from making any further remarks which are anti-Party and, for that matter, anti-German.'

Walldern's eyes narrowed as he said, 'You're not really a Nazi, Paul, you are not even a German. You're more British than you think.'

Paul had needed this break from the Army; his leave was to last a fortnight, and yet here he was on the first night heading for a violent clash with the doctor over the very roots of his existence; his love for the Nazi Party. He wondered if the doctor was merely baiting him – perhaps the Wallderns didn't want him to stay, now that they had been told the circumstances of Richard's death.

'What makes you think that I'm more British than German?'

Frau Walldern interrupted with, 'I really do think that we should go inside now – it's getting a bit chilly anyway.'

She was ignored by the other two.

'Because, Paul, for one thing you look out of place as a Nazi. That's why Nazism would never succeed in England. The dogma of the Party is so anti-individual it would never get off the ground over there. You happen to have come under its influence at a very impressionable age.'

'Surely that's the whole point, Herr Walldern. It's the youth of the country that's so important – that's why Nazism has to be taught at a young age.'

'Let me continue – you may recall that when you were here last, you said that you didn't want a war, that Hitler had said that he had no intention of declaring one. You – in fact, all of us – have been swept along with the idea. We'll all finish up being drowned!'

What's the use? thought Paul. He obviously wasn't wanted. He said, 'Herr Walldern, wouldn't it be easier to say that you don't want me to stay with you?'

The doctor sat forward in his chair as his wife said, 'Of course we want you to stay. Now the two of you, no more talk of this, please.'

The doctor rapidly agreed with his wife about Paul staying, but not about a change in the conversation, not just yet anyway.

'We want you to spend the whole of your leave with us, Paul, but I would be happy to hear your confirmation that you are not a Nazi.'

Before Paul could reply, Frau Walldern stood up and, walking towards the house, groaned to her husband, 'What's the point in going on and on about that? It won't bring Richard back. I'll see you both indoors.'

'Look, Herr Walldern, please don't—'

'No, Paul,' Walldern interrupted, 'I am an older, though not necessarily wiser, man than you, but listen to me a little longer.'

'It will be impossible to do that if you go on running down the Nazis.'

'You must listen to me,' Walldern replied abruptly. Then, in a calmer voice, he said, 'I know you will not report me, for you didn't tell the authorities about the scene you had with Frau Hofer; remember?'

'That was different. She was very upset, she didn't realise what she was saying.'

'Oh, but she did, Paul.'

'Then perhaps I will do so,' retorted Paul. But he went on, 'What happened in the end?'

'Her husband is still a sick man. The brother died in the camp at Sachsenhausen – at least that's what they were told.'

'I see – I'm sorry to hear that.'

'Yes, Paul, and so were many other people. Have you any idea of what happens in these concentration camps?'

'The same as in other prisons. I suppose they are just locked up and guarded in the normal way.'

'I thought you would say that, but when I tell you that the wretched inmates are starved, tortured, beaten and in most cases subjected to the most appalling human indignities, what would you say then?'

'That you are not telling the truth.'

'Paul, as a doctor I may do odd things from time to time. I would like to be a more patient individual, and perhaps more understanding and many other things. But there is one good point about me – I don't tell lies.'

'Then shall I just say that you have been misinformed.'

'You may not. I assure you it's the truth.' It was getting

colder now. The sun had disappeared. 'Shall we go inside now?'

As they slowly strolled across the lawn, Walldern continued, 'I don't want to upset my wife any more, so we will not talk of these matters in front of her. But I want to say finally that the Hitler regime is evil and wicked. We are a strange race, Paul, a race that is easily led. Germany did not deserve to get the government that's in power.' As they reached the house, he turned to Paul and said, 'Look at those wonderful mountains.' They both stood and felt dwarfed by the visual impact of the scene. Still looking in the distance, Walldern took Paul's arm in his hand and said, 'Evil conquers, but never triumphs.'

Chapter Thirty-two

October 1940 had been the best month of all for Paula. John Bright's first letter to his parents from Oflag VIII was heavily censored, but the details of his meeting Paul at Dunkirk were untouched. As soon as Heide had received the news from the Brights, he phoned Paula at the cottage outside Horsham – the comfortable little home her mother had bought, and which had become a haven for the family in escaping from the Blitz.

'Paula,' he had said over the phone, 'I've had news of Paul.'

'Oh, thank God!' she replied breathlessly, 'That is, if it's good news. Tell me quickly please, Mr Heide.'

Heide's affection for Paul was undiminished and the account John Bright had given of the meeting in Dunkirk brought joy to his heart. He was holding the letter in his hand as he spoke to Paula. The Brights wanted them to return it to them. It had travelled badly from Germany, its thin paper heavily crumpled. Heide held it in his hand as though it was a valuable piece of Dresden china – it seemed to be a link with Paul.

'It's good news, Paula. He's safe, or was so at the time of Dunkirk.'

'How have you heard?'

'An old school friend met him in the middle of Dunkirk. The friend was among the British captured.'

'No one is at home just now, so tell me everything.'

'There's nothing more to tell you, my dear. Except that, according to John Bright, Paul is very pro-Nazi still – that's only natural – they've had so much success.'

'Do you think he knows about the concentration camps?'

'He knows about them,' replied Heide. 'But he's probably among the many Germans who do not believe what's inside them. But how are you and young David?'

'We're both fine—' She paused. She might have added that she was very tired. Her father's opinion of Paul had now turned to a bitter hatred and he lost no opportunity of declaring his dislike. The bombing of London had made him loathe the Germans, and his nerves had suffered even more after he had experienced part of the Blitz. Paula was unable to adjust herself to the prospect of living on the bounty of her parents, and family bickering was frequent. But at least the baby was protected and cared for.

'And you, Mr Heide, how are you getting on?' she continued.

'I'm well, thank you, Paula.' He tried to hide his downcast feelings and sound happy. 'I have a translating job at the Ministry.'

'Oh, that sounds interesting,' she lied.

'Not really, but it's something to keep my mind occupied. I'm not allowed to travel outside a radius of ten miles from London. I'm lucky not to be interned still.'

'If I can get the time off, I'd love to see you in town for a day. Daddy likes you, so I could tell him.'

'Try and do that,' said Heide, and then, 'Are you still in love with Paul?'

He was glad when she said 'yes', but fearful as to how the future would ever bring happiness for them.

'Mr Heide—' her voice broke. 'Will Paul ever be with me again?' Heide could guess how close to despair she must be.

'Why not?' His brain tried to pick phrases that would comfort her. 'We all have to be patient these days. So many throughout the world are separated from their loved ones.'

Paula drew a deep breath. 'I can and will wait.' She faltered, 'I don't care who wins the war, as long as he's safe. The Germans have done some horrible things, I know, but I'm too soft to hate permanently.'

'You've put that well, Paula – and come to see me soon.'
'Where are you living?'
'Same hotel, same extravagance, I fear. I never go out in the evenings. Do you think your parents would let you stay for the night?'
'I don't know – I'll write and let you know very soon.'
They hung up.

During these days, Paula existed in a state of emptiness which might be described as living, in that she breathed, looked after David, worked in the cottage, ate and slept, but she was inwardly haunted by terrible dreams.

Two weeks after Heide's phone call she arrived at Victoria Station on a dismal and foggy London morning in mid-November.

Her depressed state of mind was made worse for Paula as the London she had left at the outbreak of war had changed to a drab, sand-bagged city. Across the river everything had looked dark and mysterious, but now, during the long wait for a taxi, she seemed to be standing alone in a changed world.

Heide was waiting for her in the hotel lounge. *How much older he looks*, she thought as he rose from his chair to greet her. He thought how charming and graceful she appeared. He placed his hands over hers and said, 'Paula, my dear girl, this is wonderful.'

'Mr Heide, I'm so pleased I could come. Mummy and Daddy both readily agreed when I asked them. They send their best wishes.'

'Thank you, Paula. Now come over here and sit down.'

She suddenly felt glad to be in London again and in the hotel where Paul had been. She sensed that at any moment he would walk into the lounge.

'Your room is booked for tonight, so you can now relax.'

'It's strange,' said Paula, 'being in London now. I hated

leaving David, and the city looked so dismal that I wanted to get the next train back to Horsham. Now we've met, though, I'm much happier.'

The lounge was full – officers from all three services gave the impression of a combined operation. Near Paula sat a senior officer of the Royal Navy, talking quietly to his wife. On the other side of them was a young pilot officer, who was obviously impressing everyone with tales of his deeds of valour.

Behind Heide sat two majors in the Army. At first their words did not reach her, but their eyes had followed her from the moment she had entered with Heide. She could see that they were talking about her. She was grateful when Paul's uncle started to talk to her again.

He had sat for some minutes looking at her and was amused, though worried, about the remarks made by the two men sitting behind him. He could hear what they were saying, and it could only be a matter of time before one of them would approach Paula. They were both on leave and anxious to get female company.

'Last night,' Heide said, 'I dreamt about you and Paul. I dreamt that the two of you were together again.' He laughed nervously. 'Everything ended happily ever after.'

Heide offered her a cigarette, and when he had lit it, she said, 'And what was the final outcome of the dream?'

'As I said, Paula, it ended happily; you both met and I was there in the background.'

'Do you believe that dreams come true?'

'Yes, sometimes they do, but you are both having the strength of your love tested. Just as you're waiting for Paul, so I'm sure that he's waiting for you.'

'Do you really believe that?'

'Yes. I was parted from my wife for long spells during the last war. Our love for each other kept us on the alert as far as any interest from the opposite sex was concerned.'

'But you were married.'

'So would you and Paul have been under normal circumstances. I think of you both as being married.'

'I've never even thought of another man. My parents often try to push unattached men on to me. Luckily the average age of men in the Horsham area at the moment is about seventy,' she laughed.

Paula's mind was perfectly clear. She knew she could wait. She wondered what Heide truly thought about Paul and the future. She sensed that he was trying to make her feel that all would be well, and yet—

'How was it that Paul became such an ardent Nazi?' she suddenly asked.

'We'll talk about that over lunch. I'll just go and make sure that a table is reserved for us.'

Now, as she watched him cross the lounge, she again noticed how age was advancing rapidly on him. *He looks more like eighty-five than a man in his late sixties.* She was still thinking about this when she heard the voice by her side.

'I say, excuse me,' it said. 'This is obviously just a pick up, but I was hoping that you might have lunch with me?'

By the middle of the sentence, Paula had realised that it was one of the Army officers who had been sitting behind Heide.

He was a pleasant-looking man, and he stood beside her fingering his short grey moustache.

Paula wrinkled her mouth at him, smiled slightly and said, 'No, I'm sorry, that's not possible.' But at the same moment she felt a certain pity for him and continued, 'London can be lonely – I'm sorry.'

'Oh – oh,' he stuttered. 'Yes, of course.' He was a shy man and it had taken a lot of courage even to approach her. 'I hope you don't think I was rude?'

'No, not at all,' and then seeing that Heide was entering the lounge, she stood up and said, 'I must go now. You will excuse me?'

As Heide helped her into her dining chair he said, 'I think I nearly lost you.'

'Yes, it was quite a fast approach. He seemed a nice man.'

'I'm sure he was, and who can blame him? You're a very pretty girl.'

Paula was glad to leave the ordering to him.

'You'll be surprised what the chef here can do with wartime rations.'

Heide felt carefree for the first time in months.

'I have booked two seats at the theatre for this evening, in the front row,' Heide said.

'The theatre – that's a great surprise! How wonderful! Thank you very much, Mr Heide.'

'I'm looking forward to it too. The times are all mixed up these days. They start and finish early because of the raids.'

Paula suddenly said, 'Do you think that Paul is still alive?'

'Alive?'

'Yes.'

'Of course he's alive.'

'Yes, but we can't be certain, can we?'

Heide wasn't hungry – he had been making an effort to eat the tinned fish which even the expert chef had, on this occasion, failed to disguise. He put his fork down and said, 'We all have the prospect of long and gloomy days ahead. Are you quite certain that you want to wait for Paul?'

She answered quickly, 'Yes.' She had also stopped eating and was now looking across the table at Heide. 'Why do you ask that?'

'Because everyone would understand if you didn't.'

'I don't really think that anyone understands, except you.'

'You would have no difficulty in finding someone.'

They were both looking intently at each other.

'I can never look into the future,' Paula said sadly.

'Ah, the future – who can tell? But we can, now and then, learn from the past.'

'Mr Heide, do you imagine that the youth of this country could have been poisoned in their minds in the same way the Nazis succeeded in doing to the young people in Germany?'

'Let's have a further go at this fish,' he suggested, and then, 'Yes, I do believe that under the same set of circumstances the same thing could have happened. Not only in this country, but all over the world.'

'In other words,' she cut in, 'when this war is over, Paul and the others in the Party out there who were too young to reason between right and wrong should be forgiven?'

Heide thought for a moment before replying.

'Yes, one would hope that would be the case. In the same way, if many of the older generations were in a hopeless situation. They too should be sympathetically treated.'

'In any case,' agreed Paula, 'people change as they go through life. Look at my father, first he disliked Paul, then he liked him, then he loathed him.'

'That is surely understandable. But you are of course correct – men and women do change. In fact, the useless men are generally those who never change with the years.'

The meal was finished in silence. On the way to the lounge for coffee Heide said, 'What would you like to do this afternoon?'

'Oh, just sit and talk – but I would like us to cheer up as Paul wouldn't want us to be so miserable.' And then, as they sat down, she added, 'Please don't talk about my finding someone else. I intend to wait for Paul, as I'm just made that way.' And then she looked Heide straight in the eyes and went on, 'I shouldn't mind if he had slept with another woman. I don't expect him to wait for me in that way. As long as he comes through the war safely, as long as he can see his son, our son, that's the most important thing in the world to me.'

Heide nodded and said, 'I shall want to make sure that he deserves you, for you're a remarkable woman.'

'I'm not that, Mr Heide, I'm just a woman. I hope that I know the true loyalty of affection. I have few real friends, and perhaps that's why Paul has always been so important to me.'

When Paula got to Horsham the next day she looked back at the time spent in London with Heide as a brief moment from which she had inwardly gained a fresh appreciation of her problems. She also felt closer to Paul than she had at any time since his departure for Germany. She was pleased about the effort the man had made to pick her up. It was good to feel that she was still attractive. She had spent much of the previous summer in the sun, playing with David in the garden. His youthful skin had tanned to a pale bronze. It had faded a little now. She hoped that when she next saw Paul it would be at the end of a summer.

Chapter Thirty-three

The Sixth Panzer regiment was in the vanguard of the attack on Russia. Hitler started on the road which he thought would lead to the domination of the world, but which ultimately led to the defeat of the Nazis.

The German Army still had absolute faith in the Führer's ability to lead them to success in any venture he decided upon. For a while the confidence was not misplaced. The attack commenced in June 1941, and by the beginning of the autumn Hitler believed that Russia was finished.

In a short space of time, within weeks, thousands of Russians had been captured and had surrendered. Paul's first contact with the Russian soldiers was with mixed feelings – part pity and part contempt. As his troop had crashed through the frontier, he had noticed that six women were in the firing line; they had put up a better defence than the men. Many of the women were killed fighting at their posts; many of the men had come forward with arms raised in the sign of surrender, clutching any white material they had been able to lay their hands on. It was only much later that Paul would begin to experience the fighting qualities of the Russian solder, when the tide began to turn against the Germans.

'There are hundreds of the bastards packing in all round me,' he reported on his wireless.

'That's good,' replied Müller on the regimental frequency.

For weeks and weeks it was all good. But events occurred that began a series of distasteful experiences for the officers and men of the Sixth Panzer regiment. They began when the

Nazi political agent arrived at Müller's headquarters, when the campaign was about a month old.

'I have come direct from Divisional Command and, as with the other regiments, you are to carry out my orders.'

Müller had taken an instant dislike to the man and almost immediately decided to be as uncooperative as possible.

'And what are those orders?' replied Müller curtly.

'All the able-bodied men and women are to be formed into forced labour groups and they will sweat their guts out for us. They must be ordered to make for our rear lines, where my men are ready to receive them.'

Müller answered angrily, 'I am a soldier – I fight other soldiers. As far as civilians are concerned, my only interest in them is that they are prevented from getting in our way; that they should be allowed to continue with the task of living as quickly as possible.'

'That is exactly what we intend doing, Colonel,' sneered the agent. 'Whether they live or not is of no concern to the Führer, but while they are alive they will work for us. I suggest that these orders are carried out as quickly as possible. I can assure you that they come direct from our leader.'

From this beginning, the savage and barbarous treatment of the Russians grew, and as it grew, so did Paul's state of confusion about the Nazis. Perhaps if his regiment had been commanded by a Nazi the doubts in his mind would never have taken shape. But Müller took every opportunity to complain in front of his officers about the uncivilised, ruthless and brutal behaviour of many of his countrymen, particularly the SS. After the capture of Kiev, the vicious acts of cruelty were intensified. Colonel Müller ignored the orders regarding the herding of civilians into groups. He would not tolerate such action and because of the speed of the advance, his disobedience went unnoticed. But nonetheless, the occasions were numerous when Paul saw the terrible methods of the SS. In a village south of Kiev, he saw the few remaining elderly people and children herded into trucks for transportation to the rear lines, where he knew they would be forced to work. Why weren't they left alone? he often wondered, and what possible use could they be?

Paul saw the sad young face of a woman in the same village. His troop of tanks had been sent to the road approaching from the south, in order to repel any counterattack. He had halted his tanks beside a small shop. The woman was standing in its entrance. He got down from the tank turret and went across to her. His first thought was how like Paula she looked – the Paula he had left, but who constantly invaded his thoughts.

'Cigarette?' he said. The woman nervously took it from him and while he lit it for her she looked into his eyes. As she inhaled the smoke she coughed, and Paul was just turning round to leave her when she clutched his arm and indicated that she wanted him to follow her into the shop.

He looked back at his troop and he felt he should call across to his tank commanders to accompany him.

She was now pulling at his arm, so he followed her through the tiny rooms and out again into a back garden.

She pointed to the far end, where, on a tree in the corner, he saw the body of a man hanging from the tallest of its branches. The woman started to whimper and then to cry out loud, indicating to Paul that she wanted the body cut down from the tree. As Paul reached the body, he guessed from its young face that it was the woman's husband. He cut through the rope, and as the body fell to the ground the woman ran forward and clasped its head in her lap. He left her there at the end of the garden and returned to his tank. Perhaps the man had committed suicide, he didn't know, but he couldn't forget the woman's sad face and the way it had reminded him of Paula.

It was only much later that night that he learned the man had been hanged by the SS troops who had captured the village. Colonel Müller had confirmed this at his nightly conference with his officers.

'Gentlemen, I have been in contact with the officer commanding the SS regiment that captured this village. He is proud that it fell with little or no casualties, and he gives complete support to the ruthless actions of his men.' And then, turning to Paul, he continued, 'The man they hanged had punctured the tyres of a Volkswagen.'

Colonel Müller continued with his orders for the next day and when these were completed he returned to the conduct of the SS troops fighting in their sector.

'There would seem to be no doubt that until the Russians are defeated, the war in their country will be bitter and bloody.' Müller's eyes swept from one face to another quickly and he gave the impression that he was addressing each officer individually. 'Therefore,' he went on, 'the sooner we finish this campaign the better. High Command has informed me that we will win by the end of this year.'

The morale of the officers was high, and they greeted the colonel's words with enthusiasm. A young captain even stood up, clicked his heels and shouted 'Heil Hitler'.

Ignoring this outburst, Müller continued in a serious tone, 'While respecting the views passed to me from above, my own are somewhat different. Providing we do not have to suffer the rigours of a Russian winter, all may be well. If we do have to put up with a Russian winter, then the situation will be much grimmer for us. I expect this to happen and we will therefore start training for such conditions as soon as the opportunity allows.'

The keenness of the officers suddenly appeared dampened as Müller finished with the words, 'You are beginning to feel the effects of stronger resistance from the Russians. As we penetrate their country, this will become even stronger. We will beat them, have no fear of that, but I give this warning that it will not be as easy as it has been so far. But whatever the circumstances, there will be no ill treatment of civilians as far as this regiment is concerned.'

Orders were then given for the following day's battle and the officers returned to their men. Paul put the instructions and orders of Colonel Müller to his troop. When he finished he asked if they had any questions.

Paul's troop were a mixed crowd. Every man came from a different part of Germany, but he had welded them into an efficient fighting unit – there had been no serious casualties, and his ability to see them safely through a battle had earned him high respect from them. They had no questions to ask and were supremely happy to do as they were ordered.

However, as they dispersed to their tanks, Paul asked his sergeant to remain behind. Sergeant Halder had joined Paul's troop a month before the invasion of Russia. Back home in Munich he had a beautiful Austrian wife. They had met skiing in the Alps the year before the outbreak of war. As soon as Paul discovered this, he had remembered his own meeting with Paula, but he had said nothing. From the man's indifference to Hitler, Paul had soon realised he was not an ardent Nazi, but this had not seemed to matter, for the sergeant's handling of the men was superb. An understanding and friendship had grown between the two. In the tank regiments during battles the officers slept, ate and drank with their men. Here, there was no distinction of a Mess – and since Richard's death, Paul had not made another close friend among the officers.

Now Paul wanted to talk to him, without the distinction of rank.

'You heard about that body I was shown this afternoon, Sergeant?'

'Yes, sir, I did. Is it true that our troops did it?'

'Yes – the SS. The man they hanged had punctured the tyres of a Volkswagen.'

In the distance they could hear the sound of gunfire, but standing by Paul's tank the two men ignored it. The sergeant said, 'If the situation were different I would like to say what I really felt, sir.'

'What situation?'

'The fact that you are an officer – because of that I cannot speak my mind.'

There was an awkward pause. Then Paul replied, 'It depends what you want to talk about.'

The sergeant remained silent for a moment and then said slowly, 'Perhaps you could tell me what you wanted to talk about, sir.'

'Oh, I just wanted to have a chat with you.' They strolled away from the tank. 'There's no need to have any guard duty tonight. There will be no Russians for miles near here.' They were now in the main street of the village, which was filled with slow-moving supply trucks.

'Just as well we have air superiority, Sergeant: these trucks would all vanish with one strafe from a squadron of planes.'

They moved back towards their tanks and then Paul said suddenly, and without looking at Halder, 'Did you know that I was born in England, that in fact I was a British subject before I became a naturalised German?'

With wide, surprised eyes Halder replied, 'No, sir, no. I didn't know that.'

Paul produced some cigarettes and they both lit one. It was the first time since Richard's death that he had spoken of his background to a stranger. He went on, 'I felt certain, and for that matter I still am sure, that Germany was the best country for me.' Paul then told Halder of his education in England and of his training in the Hitler Youth Movement, and finally about his uncle Heide. When he had finished Halder asked him, 'Do you now consider yourself a Nazi or a German, sir?'

Paul was caught off his guard by this question – he knew that he should have replied immediately that there was no difference. Six months ago he would have been angered by the question, even six weeks, or days, ago. But now he found that he was hesitating where before he had always been so sure. Wanting time to think, Paul returned the question.

Halder was anxious to make the correct answer but he was very unsure of Paul's opinion. During the few months that had passed since he joined Paul's troop Halder had developed a great admiration for his young leader, but he knew from the many occasions that the Führer was mentioned that Paul, if not ardent, was surely enthusiastic about the Party. Halder's own mind had been made up three years back when, in the centre of Munich one summer evening, a party of stormtroopers had been engaged in the usual pastime of Jew baiting. Somehow Halder had been mistaken for a Jew – he had been taken down to a dark alley off Schillerstrasse, one of the main roads leading into the square, and in spite of his protestation of innocence and his repeated denials that he was a Jew, he had received a cruel and vicious beating. Halder had loathed the Nazis since that day, not only for the physical violence inflicted, but also for the way in which the thugs had been allowed to completely dominate the police to whom Halder had complained the next day.

To Paul, Halder had said, 'I am a German, sir; I love my country, and to prove that, witness my present position. I could have stayed in my job at Munich, as it was a reserved occupation.'

'Yes,' agreed Paul, 'I did know about that.'

He was going on to say that his question had not been answered when Halder broke in with, 'Did you like the time you spent in England?'

Paul nodded slowly and said, 'Yes, yes, on reflection I did. I haven't really thought about it much. There is something very pleasant about the country, particularly London and the South. That's where I was while in the state.' *Why did I call it a state?* he thought. His mind was confused The effect of the young Russian woman's face, and its likeness to Paula, had deeply disturbed his mind. Thoughts had been flashing in on him ever since. The pointless hanging of her husband had shocked him, and the colonel's attitude had further troubled him. Who was right in this war? The Germans were going to win, of that he was certain. And yet England had not yet been defeated.

'We must remember, Sergeant Halder,' continued Paul, 'that the Führer has succeeded in everything he set out to achieve.'

Halder said, 'I didn't want to join the Youth Movement.' He hesitated, and pinched out the end of his cigarette. 'My father was against my joining. Finally I had no choice. My headmaster at school firmly believed in the objects of the Movement; I was forced to join.'

'That was good.'

'Was it, sir?' They both looked across towards some of their men who were preparing a late meal behind one of the tanks.

'My foster uncle didn't want me to join – he was probably like your father – that generation doesn't want to move with the times.'

'My father is about the same age as the Führer.'

'Meaning?'

'That they are the same generation, sir.'

It's time this conversation stopped, thought Paul, but he said, 'We are the master race now. There's little doubt but that we will conquer the world.'

'And then, sir?'

'Then the benefits of National Socialism will spread throughout it.'

'And what of the peoples who continue to oppose us?'

Paul knew the answer should have been, 'They will be destroyed'. Why didn't he say just that? Instead, he muttered, 'There are millions of socialists in the world; they will convince the others of its good.'

What have I got to lose? mused Halder. *Lieutenant Heide*

would have stopped the conversation by now had he wanted to. Perhaps he has doubts? I'll speak my mind. 'I don't believe other socialists rule by fear,' he said.

'You're talking nonsense now, Sergeant. Life goes on because of fear. Men work for fear of losing their jobs, their women love them for fear of losing them, you and I carry out our orders for fear of punishment if we disobey.'

'I don't think your men think that way about you, sir.'

Paul answered quickly, 'What do you mean, they don't think that way about me?'

'They obey you because they respect you. They're not frightened of you, sir, but they have confidence in your skill and aptitude as a leader.'

Paul was flattered – he liked Halder's way of putting things – but he had also begun to realise, at first subconsciously, but now with awareness, that his school in England, St Peter's, had developed and encouraged this type of leadership.

He said, 'We must get some sleep. Arrange for calls at five in the morning.'

'Yes, sir. Goodnight.'

'Goodnight, Sergeant.' Paul slept at the rear of his tank with his crew. In his nightmare he saw Paula being hanged by his uncle Heide, and in the background he could see Richard laughing.

Chapter Thirty-four

The Russian winter of 1941 set in, and with it came Stalin's order of the day to his troops 'Not a step back.' The German invaders began to feel the effects of the growing resistance. They started to pay dearly in lives for their gains in battle.

Stalin's rallying call to his nation was quickly taken up and he announced that 'every Russian soldier must be ready to die the death of a hero rather than neglect his duty to his country'. As the German supply lines outstretched themselves and regular deliveries of the thousand and one requirements of a modern Army became more problematic, so at the same time did the Russians begin to fight back.

Hitler's promise to his troops that the war would be over by the end of 1941 was soon broken and the Germans fought for every mile of their advance. As the winter progressed, the bitter cold played havoc with men and machines. For nearly three months the temperature was rarely above minus 50 centigrade, and was often between minus 30 and minus 40 degrees.

At this time the rapid advance towards Sebastopol commenced. The Sixth Panzer regiment was again in the vanguard of the attack and in May 1942 those troops were among the first to enter Kharkov. The fight for existence against an equally ruthless and bitter foe resulted in even Colonel Müller turning a blind eye towards the many atrocities committed by the SS troops.

It was in Kharkov that the regiment, for the first time since the invasion of Russia, was able to establish a reasonable standard of living for its men. Within a short time houses and hotels were taken over and turned into living quarters for the troops. Regimental headquarters and the officers' Mess were established in a well-built hotel in the undamaged part of Sumskaya Street, the main street of Kharkov.

Müller's regiment was also granted a period of well-earned rest and an opportunity for the men to lick their wounds. These had been considerable in terms of both men and tanks, but Paul had once again seen his troop through the battles safely and without any casualties. Decorations began to arrive. Paul received the Iron Cross and Sergeant Halder the highest award granted to other ranks.

In spite of language difficulties, the Russian civilians in Kharkov accepted the fact of German occupation quickly enough, and at first many of them cooperated with the enemy.

Russian staff were employed in the Officers' Mess and one of them, a jovial-looking Ukrainian, became very popular. He was called Chekhov and 'was nicknamed 'Chekie'. What he lacked in efficiency in the Mess he made up for by cheerfulness. Within a week, he was also operating successfully on the black market.

Paul was the only one who was able to make some kind of language contact with 'Chekie'. He did this by bewilderingly flailing his arms and speaking a mixture of German, English and some sort of lingua franca. Paul found that Chekie had a delightful sense of humour and an intense dislike of the Communist Party. He took Chekie to a corner of the Mess after dinner at the end of the first week.

'Stalin good man,' said Paul, and at the same time he circled his hand round the back of his head to indicate a halo.

Chekie pulled a long face and indicated his dislike of Stalin by drawing a quick sketch of the dictator and then using the paper to rub up and down his bottom. Chekie joined Paul in the hearty laughter at the shared joke.

It did not take long to discover that Chekie's father had

been deported to Siberia three years previously for opposition to the Communist regime.

On behalf of the rest of the Mess, Paul then indicated the need for alcoholic drinks. As soon as Chekie realised what was wanted he grinned and almost ran out of the room.

Colonel Müller had been watching Paul and called him across as soon as the Russian left.

'What was all that about?' he asked.

'I found out that he hates Stalin, sir. He seemed pleased that we have occupied the country.'

'We've a long way to go before that happens. What else did you discover?'

'Nothing much more, sir, except that he has a very happy disposition. He also knows where to find some drink. That's where he's gone now.'

A while later, Chekie appeared at the door of the Mess. Paul followed him to the entrance of the commandeered hotel. He had never seen so many bottles of vodka – at a quick glance he reckoned there were about three hundred of them.

Chekie just stood there smiling. Occupation money had not yet been issued, but eventually the Russian agreed to accept thousands of German cigarettes for the vodka.

Within two more days the Russians had helped to open the first night club in the city. Paul went there on his own, for he felt the need of a woman's company. The club was filled with German officers, each with a woman, but Paul's eyes were drawn towards the dancer who was at that moment performing a slow Russian Slavonic dance in the centre of the floor.

She was a tiny little thing with a small white painted face and a mass of dark curls. She completed her dance and walked over towards Paul, who had stood by the bar watching her.

He was delighted to find that she spoke a little German. Paul took her over to an empty table and they sat down with their drinks. She didn't talk much but sat and drank steadily. Paul tried to talk to her but he found that she only had one topic of conversation – her legs. It was so important that she didn't strain her muscles, for she had to earn her living from her legs. Did he find them pretty? Of course, but Paul suddenly was not sufficiently interested to hear any more.

He stood up, with the intention of leaving. She asked him to sit down again.

'Why are you so serious?' he asked.

She smiled. 'You may call me Mia.'

'All right, Mia. My name's Paul.'

'You are going to conquer the whole of Russia?'

'Yes, we will do that.'

'Your people cannot be more cruel than the Communists. I think you will be welcomed by most of the country.'

'We hope so,' replied Paul.

'You are married?'

'No,' he replied curtly. Behind her he saw a German kissing his girl in the back of her neck. He found that Mia had moved to his side. He noticed her curls were bleached – they smelled of musk – and they were much too close to his face. She pressed herself against him and looked up at him with bold, eager eyes. Paul thought how heavily powdered her face was and the lipstick was flaking off her mouth.

He suddenly remembered Paula and the day they had spent on the river. He had put his arms around Mia's shoulders but now he gently disengaged them.

She said that she had to change before her next dance and asked him if he would wait for her. 'Yes,' he lied. As soon as she had disappeared from view he got up and quickly left the club.

When he got back to the Mess, Chekie was still on duty.

'Vodka?' Chekie suggested.

'Thank you,' Paul replied, indicating that he wanted a large one.

'Russian women no good,' Paul said in German to Chekie as he returned with the drink.

Chekie had not understood Paul and he just stood beside him grinning.

'Russian women no good,' repeated Paul and then he used his hands to indicate the shape of a woman. He then pointed to Chekie, hoping he would realise that he was trying to refer to Russian women. It did not have this effect, for the Russian merely laughed more and wagged his finger at Paul.

It was the next morning that Paul and the other officers of the regiment were told that the rest period was to be short-lived. At the daily conference of officers, Colonel Müller announced that the regiment had been ordered to prepare for an immediate move towards the front line.

Three days later, the Sixth Panzer regiment was again in the vanguard of the German attack in its move towards Stalingrad.

Chekie had looked very sad when Paul told him the regiment was leaving. Paul had indicated to the man that he would see him again when he returned to Kharkov on leave. The Russian hadn't really understood, but he had been very pleased with the treatment he had received in his first contact with the Germans. He had previously, along with the other inhabitants, been told by the Russian authorities how terrible the treatment would be. Four days after the departure of Paul's regiment the German occupation of Kharkov began in earnest, with the military zone coming under the direct control of the Gestapo, and soon afterwards Chekie and thousands of other Russians in the city came to realise how much the authorities had underestimated how bad their treatment would be – for the Nazis embarked on a reign of terror throughout the city. The Germans on the front lines knew nothing of this – they still imagined themselves glorious victors of the Fatherland, and most of them were hoping for a speedy conclusion to the war and a return to their native land.

* * *

THE TRIUMPH OF LOVE AND LIBERTY

By 11 July 1942 the Germans were one hundred or so miles east of Stalingrad. Two months later, they were on the outskirts of the city. They were to get no further, even by mid-November. Stalin had poured in every available man to prevent the fall of the city, and for the first time since the outbreak of war the Germans were to return to the type of stalemate in battle epitomised by the trench warfare during the Great War.

The difference was that in Stalingrad, trenches were few and far between. It was the fighting yard by yard in the houses and buildings of the city that led to the same type of casualties as in the earlier war. Thousands upon thousands of men on both sides were killed daily.

The Sixth Panzer regiment reached the outskirts of Stalingrad among the leading waves of German infantry. The soldiers were battered and held at bay by the defiant Russians. The more the Russians were able to contain the Germans, the higher their confidence and morale became.

The first reaction of the invading Germans to this resistance was one of shocked surprise. But the Führer's promise that the Russians would be defeated by Christmas was held on to, and the will to fight and finish the battle as soon as possible was strong.

Just before the first attack on the city, Müller's adjutant was killed. Müller promoted Paul to the rank of captain and immediately appointed him as the replacement adjutant.

'You are going to see a lot more of me now, Captain Heide,' Müller remarked to Paul.

'I'm very sorry to leave my troop, sir. They seemed a bit upset too.'

'I expect they were,' replied Müller. 'But now you will see at first hand the problems that are thrust upon us from above.'

'When do you think we will capture Stalingrad, sir?'

'I wish I knew, Heide. It's a question that's worrying us all. Our lines of communication are very stretched. The Army commander Von Paulus told us the other day that he is far from happy with our supply situation.'

The Führer will not let us down, sir.

'Let's get that straightened out first, shall we, Captain Heide?' Müller's face seemed almost full of hatred as he went on. 'Since—' He paused and then repeated. 'Since Herr Hitler took over full command of this Army two months ago, things have started to go badly for us.'

'But, sir, surely—' interrupted Paul; he got no further.

'Just stop for a moment, Heide. I'm not very pleasant when I'm angry, as you've no doubt discovered. Now shut up and listen to me. We could have taken Stalingrad with ease over a month ago. But at that moment, Hitler in his great wisdom decided to split our forces by sending a large number of our men south to capture the Caucasus oil fields. By that time the Russians had massed the forces here in Stalingrad whom we are now trying to defeat.'

As Müller had stopped, Paul thought he could make a comment and started to say, 'But there is now the possibility—'

Again, Müller told him to shut up and said, 'High Command is of the opinion that we should retreat and re-establish much stronger lines of communication before we advance any further. Hitler has said no – we must take this city at all costs now. We shall see, Captain Heide. For my part, I order you now to make no mention of Hitler in front of me.' Seeing Paul's shocked expression, he went on, 'For your further information, what I have told you is what Von Paulus told us yesterday at the meeting I attended with other commanding officers.'

How far away to Paul seemed the days of the Youth Movement when such words would have been reported as treason. In his efforts to keep his troop and himself alive and to be thankful at the end of each day to have achieved this, Paul had taken the infallibility of his leader for granted. The Führer could never be wrong – he had achieved so much, and nothing could now stop him. Colonel Müller must be wrong, of that he was certain. Paul even thought that perhaps he was suffering from battle fatigue, and for a moment he felt it might be his duty to report this. To whom, though? The Nazi Party didn't seem to exist out here in Stalingrad.

Chapter Thirty-five

The German soldiers in the 'cauldron', as Stalin so aptly named the trap laid for them, would undergo a period of intense suffering. But on the morning after Paul's promotion, all this was still a few weeks away.

The Russian War Council of the Stalingrad Front had issued its famous order: 'The enemy must be smashed at Stalingrad.' The first effective move was the complete encirclement of the city by the Russians.

Paul was the first in his regiment to hear the news about the supply situation. He had sent over the field lines his regiment's request for petrol and ammunition. Food hadn't even been mentioned as it was thought obvious that the usual amount would be sent. He was speaking to the senior staff officer at Divisional Headquarters.

'I don't understand you, sir,' he had said.

'It's perfectly clear. The Russians have cut across our supply lines and there is no more petrol. We are sending up ammunition, but food is being strictly rationed."

Paul hurried out of his office in the basement of the nearly wrecked building which was being used as Müller's headquarters. Müller was in the turret of his tank, getting the latest reports from his squadrons. Paul clambered up the side of the tank and started to tell Müller the news.

'I can't hear a word from you out there – come inside the tank.'

When he was told of the situation, Müller smiled and said, 'That doesn't really make much difference. Our tanks are useless in this street fighting. We are being hemmed in all the time. It won't be long now before we're joining the infantry and ditching our tanks.'

'But, sir, how is it that the situation has deteriorated so quickly for us?'

'We've been cut off – it's as simple as that. Did you get any news about a conference for me?'

'Nothing at all, sir.'

'All right, Heide, you return to your snug hole. I'll join you there.'

By the time Müller rejoined Paul, messages from Headquarters were coming in fast and furious. 'About the only sense that can be made out of all this, sir,' said Paul to Müller, as he handed the colonel a vast pile of messages, 'is that the only good supplies we can get will be ammunition. It's the one item they seem to possess in plenty.'

'That means that at least we can go on fighting until relief arrives.' Müller walked over to his desk. Like Paul, he had three days' growth of beard and looked haggard. 'We are also getting reports about the Russians' treatment of our prisoners. They are far from pleasant, Captain Heide. They will murder your mother and stand you a drink of vodka afterwards.' Müller looked across at Paul and continued, 'In fact, not unlike the behaviour of our SS troops, eh, Captain Heide?'

Paul said nothing. An orderly brought over another message to him. 'It's the notification of the conference at Headquarters you were expecting, sir. In two hours' time.'

'Arrange the transport for me, Heide. That means in three hours or so, you and the rest of the regiment will know the worst.'

Paul had arranged for the squadron leaders to gather at Müller's HQ by the time the colonel returned from his conference. They all stood as Müller entered, grim faced. He smiled coldly at them and told them to sit down.

'Well, my friends,' he started, 'the situation is indeed serious. We are completely cut off and our supply lines have been well and truly cut. However, General Manstein is hoping to break through to us from the south.'

'And so, Colonel,' said the senior squadron leader, 'what are our orders?'

'Our orders are to hold our present line in this suburb until help arrives. You will be interested to know that the whole of our General Von Paulus's Army is now in this position. In other words, there are two hundred thousand of us involved. I believe that if General Manstein is unsuccessful then an attempt will be made by us to break out.'

'Can that not be attempted now, sir?' suggested Paul.

'I was told at the conference that Von Paulus had asked Hitler's permission to do this some days ago. It was immediately refused.' Müller looked from one face to another to let the effect of this sink into their minds. 'This of course means that Hitler has decided that there will be no retreat from our present positions.'

In the days that followed, Hitler would in no way relent. For the German soldiers in the cauldron, conditions became almost unbearable. It was very cold, with a temperature of minus 25 degrees Celsius. Food was scarce, uniforms and boots were worn out, and for the first time morale in the ranks sank low. To add to their miseries came the news that no winter clothing would get through to them.

By the second week of December, Colonel Müller received what at first seemed better news. There was talk of an airlift that would drop supplies over the German lines. But even this came to nothing.

Like thousands of other Germans, Paul could not bring himself to believe what was happening and that the Führer would let them down.

Colonel Müller saw how depressed his young adjutant had become. 'Do you wish you had stayed in England?' he asked

Paul one evening. Paul looked up from his desk. *God how the boy has aged*, thought Müller.

'I don't know, sir. I don't know anything much now. I just feel that we have been let down.'

'Let down?' shouted Müller. 'Out there in the snow my men are reduced to living on four ounces of bread and a little horse flesh, if they're lucky.' Paul looked at Müller and saw that he wasn't directing his eyes towards him, he was gazing at the ceiling. Müller went on as if he were talking to himself. 'They're freezing to death! For Hitler.' He covered his face with his hands. 'We can no longer attack, but just wait and try to repel the Russians when they come.' He looked at Paul. 'It can't last much longer.'

An orderly brought a message over to Paul. He read it with blank and staring eyes and passed it to Müller. The colonel took it without looking at Paul.

It was a copy of the order of the day, sent from Hitler's HQ. General Von Paulus had instructed that it be sent to all commanding officers for their attention and action.

Müller's tired eyes spelled out each word. He threw it back to Paul and said, 'No, you read that out loud.'

'I have read it, sir.'

'I said read it out *loud*!' Müller shouted the last word.

Paul held the message in his hand and found his frozen fingers were shaking. ' "Surrender is forbidden!" ' He read on, ' "The German Army in Stalingrad will hold their positions to the last man and the last round and by their heroic endurance will make an unforgettable contribution towards the establishment of a defensive front and the salvation of the western world." '

Paul had finished reading the message.

'That's your glorious Führer for you,' said Müller. ' "The western world," he says. It was only a short time ago that you and I were fighting against that world in France! The man's mad.'

Paul said nothing. He looked at Müller and saw that tears were pouring down his face. He heard him mutter, 'Oh my God, my poor country. Where is this madman leading us?'

The wireless and telephone operators in the far corner of the room had their backs to Colonel Müller but they could hear his sobs. Paul went to Müller's side and murmured, 'How about some sleep for you, sir. Please let me help you.' Paul took Müller's arm and led him to the tiny anteroom which served as his bedroom.

Müller dropped onto his camp bed and looking up at Paul said, 'Thank you, Captain Heide. Call me immediately I'm required.'

The impact of events was bearing down on Paul. He began to recall arguments he had had in the past with Heide, with Richard's father, and with the others who had opposed Hitler.

As he sat down, he saw the operators and orderlies looking at him.

'The colonel will soon be back. Carry on with your work.'

He convinced himself that the Führer would find a way out for his Army that was trapped in Stalingrad. When that happened, all his critics would be fighting to be the first to say how great their leader was.

He spoke aloud to the silent soldiers who turned to listen. 'Colonel Müller is a very tired man. He will be better after a rest, and I'm sure I can rely on you not to talk of what you've heard and seen.'

They could all hear the artillery fire which had been going on continuously for nearly a week now. The troops were used to this, but the bitter cold and lack of food were taking their toll on the men's health and courage and will to fight on.

Paul went up the stairs from the basement dugout, walked past the guards, and then went out into the street. The guards outside were cowering and shivering in the shelter of debris, and at the end of the street he could see the three Panzer IV tanks. They were lined abreast across the street. When they were destroyed, there would be nothing left for the defence of the headquarters.

He looked up to the tops of the buildings. All their roofs had been torn off. A section of weary infantry passed on their way to battle positions on the streets a mile or so ahead. They were all unshaven and blankets were draped over their shoulders. They marched out of step and each pair of eyes told of the misery being suffered by their bodies.

One of the men carried a dead dog on his shoulders – it would be skinned and cooked for the evening meal.

The city was wrapped in a pall of smoke. Paul saw that it had started to snow again.

'Can't you see that I've always waited for you, Paul.' Paula was standing outside that little restaurant in London where they had said goodbye.

He moved towards her, but as he did so she stepped away. She turned and ran and he chased after her. Round the next corner he stopped. Paula had reached the end of the street but had turned back and was now running towards him. She was carrying a child in her arms. He saw his uncle behind her and heard him shouting at her to stop.

The screech of a bomb came so near that it seemed to be inside Paul's head. Then the world fell to pieces as it exploded between him and Paula.

'Paula!' he screamed. 'Paula come back – Paula!' He felt the hand shaking his shoulder and then he heard the orderly's voice.

'Sir, wake up, sir, quickly, wake up! Headquarters want you on the phone.' Paul's tortured bloodless face with feverish burning eyes looked at the orderly as he came out of his nightmare. He staggered to his desk and picked up the receiver.

Chapter Thirty-six

The staff officer speaking to Paul had a high-pitched voice. This gave a higher note of panic to his voice as he spoke.

'Is the colonel there?'

'Yes,' replied Paul, 'but he's resting at the moment, sir. Do I have to disturb him?'

'I should speak to him, but there is not time. I have all our units to contact. Briefly the situation is this. General Manstein has failed to break through to us. Our only hope now is that this can eventually be achieved. In the meantime, our present positions are to be held – there must be no retreat. These are Hitler's orders! There will be no written confirmation of these orders. Are they understood?'

'Yes – yes, they are understood, sir.'

There did not seem to be any necessity to awaken Colonel Müller. There was nothing new in the orders. Paul sat at his desk staring at the notes he had taken. He remembered his dream of Paula. For the first time he felt he would never see her again. He had fallen in love with her at first sight but his love for Hitler had been stronger. He remembered the time they had spent together at Arosa and their meeting in London. The time he showed her over St Peter's. St Peter's – he began to think of his days there, of the English, their way of life and the people he had met. He compared them with the Germans and considered now that there didn't seem to be much difference. Perhaps the English had their SS types too, only they didn't show on the surface.

He looked up from the desk and saw Colonel Müller standing at his doorway looking back at him. Paul stood up and saluted. 'Are you feeling more refreshed now, sir?'

'Yes, thank you, Captain Heide. As a matter of fact, I've been standing here some minutes watching you. You looked very deep in thought.'

'Yes, sir.' Paul bent down and picked up the notes he had taken during the call from Headquarters. 'There is a message for you – can we discuss it in your room?'

When they were in Müller's room, Heide said, 'I think you will agree that it is best that the orderlies do not hear this.'

Paul passed on the orders he had been given. Müller had sat down on his bed. 'Did the men out there hear what I was saying before you brought me in here?'

'No, I don't think so, sir. Does it matter much if they did?'

'No, no.' Müller beckoned to the small stool by his bed and told Paul to sit down. 'Captain Heide, does the thought of death worry you?'

Paul hesitated and then answered, 'Yes – yes, it does. I don't want to die.'

'You realise, don't you, that we cannot last much longer. Then it will be up to the Russians. They may not want to take any prisoners.'

'That had occurred to me.'

'What are your views on Hitler now?'

Paul didn't answer the question. Colonel Müller continued, 'It may be difficult for you to comprehend, but I know now that Germany has lost this war.'

'That's a sweeping statement, sir, just because we're losing a battle.'

'We're going to lose two hundred thousand men because of Hitler's stupidity, and that will take some getting over. It is the beginning of the end for Germany. We are going to lose the war because we now have the world against us.'

'But the fighting ability of our armies will stand up against the whole world.' As soon as Paul said that, he remembered the poor wretches he had seen going up to the line. What a contrast to the Army that had defeated France!

'Oh yes, you're right there. We will fight to the bitter end I imagine – just as we are doing here – but we will lose.'

Paul had a moment of insight. He knew the colonel was right. Sometimes at St Peter's during a rugby match there was a moment, and it would often come before the end of the first half, when he knew on that day the opposition would win.

'What were you thinking about when I came into the room a moment ago?'

'I had a short sleep, sir. I had a dream about my girl in England. I was thinking about her, I suppose.'

Müller glanced at Paul and said, 'I hope you get through this war safely. Will you stay in Germany if you do?'

'I don't know. I feel a great bond has been built up in me in the Army, particularly in this regiment. The German soldier has been a wonderful man to lead, as good as any soldier in the world.'

'When it's all over you should write a book, Captain Heide. I cannot think that there are many other Englishmen who have done the same things as you.' Müller looked at Paul and went on, 'Our country will be hated when this war is finished. It will need someone like you to tell the world that not all Germans are bastards!'

Müller stopped talking for a long moment and then stood up. 'I don't for a second believe that you have got Adolf Hitler out of your system yet, but if you live you are going to – remember that. It will be up to people like you to see that such a man never gets power in Germany again. Come along now, Captain Heide, we must go out and visit the poor devils on the front line.'

Paul found himself meekly following Müller. He was disconcerted by the fact that he had not said one word in defence of the Führer.

As the food and ammunition ran out, the directives to all German units from Staff Headquarters to fight on increased.

Even at the last stage of the disaster, Hitler managed to make full use of his propaganda machine. From his safe shelter hundreds of miles behind the lines, instructions poured out in a flood of appeal to German patriotism.

The last written order of the day reached Müller's headquarters in the early part of January.

Paul handed the order to him. As Müller read it he grinned.

'Have you read this, Captain Heide?'

'No, sir.'

'Well, I will read it to you. And then we will tear it up.'

Before he read the order he said, 'Remember, Heide, this was sent personally by the Führer. This is the man who said he would never desert his soldiers. The man who has always laid such great stress on never being the cause of shedding a drop of German blood unnecessarily. The man who could have given the order to save us all here in Stalingrad to fight another day.' Müller's expression matched his anger. 'The order reads, "If we fall into Russian hands it would be equal to suicide. Either we will be immediately shot or we will die a slow agonising death in Siberia. We must fight to the last man and the last round." That's all it says.' Müller crumpled the paper in his hands and told Paul to put a match to it.

'The madman can't even trust us to die gallantly and as far as my regiment is concerned he's right. When the moment comes I shall order our men to surrender.'

That moment came three days later – the last rounds had been fired. Müller gave the general order for the troops under his command to surrender.

There must have been about forty Russians, Paul remembered later, who advanced down the road towards the dugout and the dirty white flag of surrender he was holding. Müller was standing by his side. Leading the Russians was an officer. He approached Müller and halted a few yards away. 'Commandant, you,' he shouted and pointed to Müller. The colonel stepped forward slowly. The two men faced each other. The Russian looked about the same age as Paul. He beckoned the colonel to walk away from him, and as Müller turned his back, the Russian aimed at it and went on firing until his revolver was empty.

Paul ran over to the body. It was quite dead, but Müller's face was wearing a contented smile. He turned and looked at the Russians. The officer waved at him to walk towards their lines. Paul made his first steps towards the Siberian camp and two and a half years of captivity.

Chapter Thirty-seven

At intervals throughout the war Erik Heide had seen Paula, but never for more than a few days at a time. In a world of broken promises, disloyalty and the widespread misery inflicted by the Nazis, Heide had been strengthened by Paula's complete devotion to Paul.

He always found it hard to believe that she was so different from the crowd. 'My dear,' he had once said to her, 'are you sure that you're not living in a fairyland?'

'I'm waiting for him, if I have to wait for ever. Our son David knows all about him.'

Heide stared at her and thought, *I'm so much older than she, yet her wisdom and faith are greater than mine.*

On every occasion when Heide sought to prepare her and reconcile her to the fact that she might never see Paul again, she always quickly killed any such thought, 'It's nonsense contemplating what may or not happen, Mr Heide,' she would cut in. 'There is nothing to contemplate. I just have the conviction that Paul and I will be together again. And when we are, we will never part.'

'You have great faith.'

'Yes, I have, but it's faith centred on God.' She paused. 'People who talk about going to church regularly are often pompous. I hope you will not think that of me.'

'No, Paula, of course not.'

'Well,' she continued, 'I go to church every Sunday – that is I go to the early-morning communion. It is by far the most beautiful service and the one with the most meaning for me.'

'Is that where you get your moral strength?'

'Yes, I suppose it is – but from the service, not from the man taking it. I made the mistake of telling him once about Paul.'

'Why was that a mistake?' asked Heide.

'Because he tried to convince me that Paul and I had committed a great sin, having David and all that.'

'Perhaps he was only trying to be helpful,' Heide suggested. 'In his eyes, you had both done wrong.'

She quickly answered, 'In his eyes, maybe, but not in God's. I couldn't believe that. God forgives our wrongs as long as we ask Him to forgive us.'

Heide was deeply touched by her confidence and hope.

He said, 'No man who deserved a worse woman ever had a better one.'

'What do you mean?'

'You and Paul.'

She was angry then. 'Please don't ever say anything like that again, Mr Heide.'

After that they had sat looking at each other for a long time without saying anything. It was Heide who broke the ice. 'Would you like to go on talking about the Church?'

'Not particularly.'

'Please do – you know I don't go to church these days. I didn't think that any young people did either.'

'I don't think many do.'

'But you do, Paula. Please go on.'

'There's nothing much else to say. I say my prayers, and try not to ask for selfish things.'

'I wonder if Paul prays,' said Heide.

'I hope he does. But if he doesn't it won't matter as I pray for him. I always start by saying, "Please God, forgive me my sins and those of Paul. Make me truthful, pure, obedient and kind."' Paula seemed to have forgotten Heide's presence, for she had closed her eyes and went on talking. '"Keep me safe and protect little David. Grant that we may all be safe together some day soon."'

She opened her eyes and went on looking straight into Heide's face, 'and then I pray for lots of other people – people I've never met, like those in any sorrow or distress. I always finish by saying, "if it be Thy Will".' She smiled. 'I believe God will answer my prayers.'

'I hope he will,' Heide said. 'What do your parents think of the future for you?'

'They never talk about Paul, of course. They've given up trying to make me forget him. Daddy realises that's a complete waste of time, thank goodness.'

'When this war is over,' Heide had once said to her, 'let us hope that a world in peace becomes the aim of all its inhabitants. A world in which we are freed from all our ills.'

Paula had agreed and added, 'May Paul have also learned his lesson. Do you imagine that he will want to live in Germany?'

Heide had smiled kindly and replied, 'My dear, let's cross that hurdle when we come to it. There are so many possibilities. I certainly hope that I can go back, even though I'm becoming an old man.'

'Considering all you've been through, I think you look marvellously young.'

After the successful allied landings in Normandy, Erik Heide had a change of work. From interpreting, he suddenly found himself involved in the department preparing for the allied occupation of Germany. He learned that a Control Commission was to be formed and that he was to be considered for a civil appointment in Hamburg. From that moment until the end of the war, Heide threw himself into his work.

The war ended in May 1945. Hitler was beaten. It was on 5 June that Heide phoned Paula and urgently requested her to come to London and see him the next day.

* * *

As she entered the foyer of the hotel, Heide noticed that Paula was trembling a little. She didn't notice that he was trembling too. Since the end of the war in Europe Paula had been in almost daily contact with Heide on the phone. But try as he might, he could get no news of Paul.

She said immediately, 'You have news?'

'Not yet about Paul, but I am going to Hamburg early next week. Now sit down and let me tell you all about it.'

She listened patiently while he explained the work he was to do in helping restore order out of the chaos in Hamburg.

She became impatient to know how this would help in finding the whereabouts of Paul, but Heide made no mention of this.

Finally she almost shouted at him, 'And Paul? What of him? You must find him!'

'My dear, you must control yourself Of course I'll do all I can to find him. But it's going to perhaps take a long time.'

'Why?'

'Now come on, Paula, calm down. We've both waited long enough for him. A few more months won't make any difference.'

Oh God! he thought. *She can't see that Paul may be dead – may have been dead for years.*

She couldn't fail to notice the huskiness of his voice as he said, 'It may be a long time before we ever find out which service he joined, let alone what part of the world he fought in. You must be patient – you know I'll do all I can to find him, don't you?'

'Yes, Mr Heide. Yes, I do.' She suddenly felt frightened. 'How long is it now – seven years, isn't it? Seven years.'

What an age it seems, she thought, and yet in some ways it seemed only yesterday when Paul had left her.

Heide didn't say anything but sat there looking at her. He remembered that he had put some notes about Hamburg in his pocket and he pulled them out.

'The city of Hamburg has had some terrible bombing. It

almost certainly means that my house has been destroyed.' She didn't seem to take any notice so he said, 'If Paul is still alive, I'm certain he will make for Hamburg.' Heide felt that the moment had come for them to talk over all the possibilities.

'*If* he's alive?' she said. 'Of course he's alive.'

'But Paula, you must be prepared for all kinds of situations.'

'I am prepared,' she replied, 'for everything, except for Paul's death. I know that he is alive.'

'But if he is alive...' Heide hesitated. 'If he is alive, can't you see he may have changed? He may even be married.'

She said nothing. Then she said, 'Why haven't you talked like this before? You've done so much to help me keep my faith all these years.'

'We all needed help to be strong,' Heide said. 'But supposing I do find him and he has not changed his views.'

'Well, there's no longer a Hitler for you to worry over, is there?'

How could he explain all his fears? Not only for Paul and Paula, but for the future. Germany and its people. Could anyone ever be sure that the Nazis had learnt their lesson, let alone that they had changed in their outlook?

Paula could see that he looked dejected and tired, as though his vitality had gone. Suddenly she said, 'What will happen to the men who were Nazis?'

He felt angry with himself now, for he realised that his pessimism was acting like a poison on her.

He said, 'We cannot yet tell what will happen to them. Perhaps it will be, as Shakespeare once wrote, "Some shall be pardoned and some punished".' He smiled at her, hoping to cheer her up with more definite plans for her. 'Will you come out to Germany if, er, *when* I find him?'

'Yes, if that's what he wants.'

'And your parents?'

'They have changed, especially Daddy. I was going to tell you. The other day he actually said to me that he wondered what had happened to Paul. I believe he seems to admire the way in which I've waited for him.'

'Well, we shall see,' Heide replied. 'We must make some plans for you. I already have one or two ideas, but they must wait for now. You understand, that don't you? The important thing is to find Paul.'

Paula smiled and said, 'Yes it is. Oh God it is.' And then, 'I wish I could do something positive to help.'

'You can help most by waiting a little longer. There's nothing else you can do at the moment. Except, of course, to look after yourself and David.' He smiled.

'I'll do that,' she agreed.

Chapter Thirty-eight

It was towards the end of June, when Heide had been in Hamburg for only two weeks, that he had his first clue that might lead him to discover the whereabouts of Paul. It was by chance during a conversation with an old German friend he had located in the city.

'I believe they have caught that Seebohm man just outside Bremen,' was all he had said. Memories flooded back to Heide of the pre-war days and Paul's frequent meetings with the man – and the visit Seebohm had made to his house on that dark night so many years before.

Heide's first week in Hamburg as assistant to the military governor was like a kind of rebirth for him. There were few of his friends still in the city, and the ones he met there seemed stunned by events. And then, when the veil was torn away from Belsen and Hitler's other terrible works, Heide and those of his remaining friends suffered an attack of repugnance from which they never quite recovered.

Germany, Heide quickly perceived, was a ruined country, morally, materially and psychologically.

Heide was still in a dazed state when he asked the governor if information could be obtained for him about the whereabouts of Seebohm.

'You see,' Heide had said, 'it is possible that the man may know what happened to my foster nephew.'

Within half an hour Seebohm had been located. Two phone calls from the military governor's office in Hamburg to his opposite number in Bremen, and the Nazi had been located in the prison already filled with men who were later to face trial at Nuremburg. Seebohm was to become known as one of the main supporters in Hitler's 'annihilation' of the Jews.

By the following afternoon, Heide had made the journey to Bremen. He was not allowed to see Seebohm on his own and throughout the interview the Nazi was flanked by two burly military policemen. Heide was sitting on one side of a long table as Seebohm was brought before him.

Heide noticed a kind of surprised uneasiness on the pale unshaven and anxious face of the man, but Seebohm had not recognised him immediately.

'Sit down. I have some questions to ask you,' Heide said casually.

Heide smothered a desire to treat Seebohm as he had once been treated by him. He remembered the night that Seebohm had called on him; the man had not changed much – he still had a powerful-looking body, his brown eyes still had that hard ruthless look – but there was something about them now that had a frightened appearance.

Seebohm sat down and quickly said, 'You are German?'

'I am the one that asks the questions now, Herr Seebohm.' For an instant Seebohm saw the look of contempt and hatred on Heide's face, but he was still truculent enough to answer back, 'I said that because I think I've met you before.'

Heide felt an urgent wish to vent his feelings on the man. Seebohm personified the evil that was Hitler in the old man's eyes, but he replied, 'Yes, we have met before. My name is Heide. I once lived in Hamburg.' Then he stopped talking and waited for the reaction of the Nazi. He didn't have to wait long, for, with a flash of recognition, Seebohm leapt to his feet and, stretching his arm across the table, made to take Heide's hand in his. He was not put off by Heide's expression or his failure to take his hand, for he said in an excited voice, 'Yes of course, of course, I knew that I had seen you before. You had the boy, the boy Paul.' Seebohm slowly sat down, his eyes never leaving Heide's.

'That was not quite correct,' went on Heide. 'You had the boy. You had him.' Heide realised now that he was faced with a tricky problem. If he did not handle the man tactfully he might not give him the information he required about Paul. Heide continued, 'This is not a meeting devised to question you on your activities in the Nazi Party. I am seeing you about a private matter.'

'I cannot understand why I have been put under arrest,' Seebohm said.

You bloody arrogant fool, thought Heide, but he said, 'That is another matter – it does not concern me. I am not here to take any statements from you or anything like that, and as I have already said, I ask the questions.'

Seebohm stared at Heide and his thoughts centred on trying to recall the details of Heide's past. But the Nazi had been responsible for so many deaths and other tragedies in individual German lives that, luckily for Heide, he could not remember the exact nature of Heide's defection from Germany.

There was an interval of silence in the room. The two guards seemed to spend all their time looking at the back of Seebohm's head. Suddenly Heide said, 'What happened to Paul?'

'I don't know.'

'Didn't you see him when he came here from England?'

'Yes.'

'I want you to tell me what happened to him when he came to Germany.'

'He was a great credit to the Führer,' Seebohm said. 'He went to an officers' training regiment – trained to be a Panzer officer. I personally always thought that a waste of the boy's possibilities.'

'What happened to him after that?' Heide tried to hide his anxiety to find Paul.

Seebohm smiled, 'Can you help me if I tell you?'

'I don't know – what do you mean "help"?'

'Get me released.'

Heide hesitated. An outright refusal might slam the door shut on any further information. He said, 'Perhaps. Now tell me, where did he go after his training?'

He joined a Panzer regiment.'

'Which one?'

'I wouldn't be able to remember that.'

'Try to.'

'Why should I?'

Seebohm felt very tired, and in any case could not recall anything more about the boy.

Heide went on, 'When was the last time you heard about Paul?'

In an instant Seebohm recollected Heide's activities. He no longer felt tired, for he suddenly almost shouted, 'You betrayed your country! I remember now.' He stood up and the two guards moved forward together and held the Nazi by his arms.

'You can put it that way if you wish – there are many other Germans who think differently,' Heide said.

Still standing and still held by the guards, Seebohm replied, 'I know nothing more about the boy. I hope that with the millions of other loyal Germans he died a glorious death for the Führer.'

Heide stood up and they faced each other across the table.

'I take it, then, that there is nothing else you can tell me.'

'Not about him.' And then his voice rose to an angry hiss. 'But I can tell you more about the future.'

'I'm going to tell the guards to take you away now. I might add that it gives me a great deal of pleasure to see you tasting a little of the medicine that you have enjoyed giving to other people over the past years. You will find, however, that the treatment you get from the British will be more civilised.'

Seebohm laughed and said, 'Let me tell you about the future. You think you have won the war – you and the

Americans – but just wait! The Russians will finish you both off. But for them, you would have lost the war. The English are finished in any case – the Americans will not be denied their pound of flesh in the years to come.'

'Take him away.' The guards led Seebohm reluctantly towards the door. On the way, Seebohm turned to Heide and said, 'You'll remember my words – the West has won a hollow victory.'

The same night Heide wrote to Paula and told her that he had made his first successful contact in his search for Paul. He could not bring himself to tell her how very far away he still was in the search.

When he had finished the letter his hands fell limply to his sides. He was tired and depressed. He wondered what would become of Germany now. And Paul, if he was still alive. Would he be like Seebohm?

He had worked for so many years after the first war ... the war to end wars ... to make Germany respected. He could not see how Germany could ever again be respected by the rest of the world. The Anglo-German Society no longer existed. The boy he had adopted had become a Nazi. His own son had been killed in the first war. He felt his work and life had been in vain. He was an old man now. Germany would be corrupt and infected as long as there were people like Seebohm. And if Paul was alive and still a Nazi... He felt a growing anger rising in him. Should he ever find him, he might want to kill him.

After several unsuccessful attempts, Paul finally escaped from the Russian prison in Siberia. He found his way across hundreds of miles of the Soviet Union until he reached the Turkish border. He made the long trek across that country to Istanbul, and from there worked his passage on a ship to an Italian port. From Italy he went directly to Hamburg.

It was August 1945. The leading daily newspaper of Hamburg had just recommenced publication under the direction of the Allied Control Commission. Paul met a reporter in a bar on the dockside and told him his story. The next day Heide read the article about Paul in the paper.

By the same evening Heide had located Paul. They met at the newspaper office. The two men faced each other – neither said anything. Paul was dressed in a mixture of Army and civilian clothes. The editor remained sitting at his desk. Heide was remembering that evening so long ago when he had last seen Paul. Paul was remembering the same moment and thinking, *He will know about Paula.*

Heide was shocked at the physical change in Paul. He hoped he wasn't showing his shock. He would have walked past him in the street. The eyes were haggard, his body so thin that it almost looked deformed. Paul's face was marked with lines which pain and suffering, rather than age, had traced across it. Neither man could believe that this was actually happening.

Heide's old eyes were full of tears, Paul's were quite dry. Suddenly, with a complete abandonment that shook his shoulders, Heide sobbed and the tears rained onto his coat lapels. Paul moved slowly towards him and put his hands on his uncle's shoulders. The editor got up and left the two alone.

Paul spoke first. 'I've come home. And so have you, Uncle.'

'I don't think,' replied Heide, stumbling over his words. 'I don't think,' he repeated, 'I can find any of the words I want. I have prayed for this moment so many times in all these years, working out what I'd say to you, and now ... now there's nothing I can say.'

Heide suddenly threw his arms round Paul's neck and hugged him.

'You haven't changed much, Uncle.'

Heide moved back from Paul a pace and said, 'You have changed,' and then, 'Has it all been hell, Paul?'

'Yes and no. I have changed, though, in almost every way that it's possible for a man to change in the space of a few years.'

Heide said, 'How long has it been?'

'Seven, eight years – it doesn't seem so long now.'

And then for some time they said nothing. Presently Paul said, 'Paula?'

'She is well.' Heide saw immediately a change of light in the young man's eyes. He continued, 'She has your son. It's been very difficult for her, but she has waited for you all these years.'

'I too have waited for her, Uncle.' He paused. 'And my son?' he asked.

'He's like you – she called him David, David John. She wanted to call him Paul, but couldn't for the sake of peace with her parents.'

'Do they hate me so much?'

'Not now,' Heide said.

'I must see her! I must see my son!' And then he almost shouted, 'Those two kept me going in the prison camp!'

'Calm down, Paul,' Heide said. 'You look ill. You must get well first.'

'I'm well enough now.'

'No, Paul, you must wait!' Heide said. 'In any case, it will not be so easy to get you to England at the moment.'

'I got back all the way from Siberia!' Paul was shouting again. 'Are you trying to stop me?'

Heide spoke sharply. 'Can't you see, Paul? You gave up your British nationality to fight for Hitler. If you go to England you will be a prisoner of war!'

'But the war is over, Uncle.'

'Yes, Paul. And I am now a member of the British Control Commission. I can help you to see Paula and your son. But you must be patient.'

Paul sank into a chair. He suddenly felt very tired. 'Yes,

perhaps you are right,' he said. 'We have already waited so long.'

Heide looked at Paul. He felt so many mixed emotions. He remembered the small English boy he had brought to Germany. Paul's own parents had not spent much time with the boy, and he had been so busy with his work he had not realised that Paul was being indoctrinated by the Nazi Youth Movement. How could he blame Paul? Perhaps all evil was brought about by the lack of love ... and lack of time to care. He should blame himself as much as Hitler.

He went over to Paul and sat on the arm of his chair. 'How did you know about your son?' he asked.

'Somewhere down the line,' Paul said, and then he remembered Bright. 'John Bright at Dunkirk. I met him at Dunkirk.'

'Yes,' Heide said. 'He was killed some years ago, trying to escape from his prisoner-of-war camp.'

'I see,' Paul said. 'There have been so many deaths. It doesn't mean anything to me any more.'

'No further talk now, Paul. Come with me.' Heide put his arm round Paul's shoulders and they stood up and walked towards the door together. Just before he opened it, Heide said, 'We'll spend the next week finding each other again.'

Chapter Thirty-nine

Through the Control Commission Heide had obtained a flat on the outskirts of Hamburg, and it was there that he took Paul. Heide's days were fully occupied with his work at the Commission's headquarters, and it was only in the evenings that he found the time to talk with Paul.

A housekeeper had been easy to find, and she also did the cooking, and Heide did his best to obtain as much food as possible.

Paul was determined to make himself fit again as quickly as possible for Paula and his son. In the weeks that followed he spent many hours wandering about the devastated city of Hamburg. The Hitler Youth Centre lay in ruins. Paul remembered his pride in working for the Youth Movement – he had been so sure, confident and trustful of Hitler. It was a stranger's city to him now. All his decorations for gallantry meant nothing. His Iron Cross was another cross to bear.

There were no familiar faces in the city, and the British Army was everywhere to be seen. Paul felt himself isolated from the English voices he overheard in the streets. He remembered his childhood in England. Had Brighton been Blitzed? And St Peter's School? Did London lie in ruins, as Goering has claimed? What had been the point of it all?

It was the contrast in Paul that continued to upset Heide. From being strong and alive, he now seemed dead. Like Germany. There were so many pieces to put together. How would Paula react? He still had not told her that Paul had come back. He had told Paul that he was arranging for Paula to come very soon. Paul trusted him. Heide was afraid for all of them.

His talks with Paul sometimes went on into the early hours of the morning. Heide was still not sure about Paul and his true feelings.

One evening he said to Paul outright, 'Have you given up being a Nazi?'

Paul looked at his uncle. How could he describe the way he felt? He said slowly, 'I am no longer a Nazi. I think that I can truthfully say that this occurred two and half years ago at Stalingrad.'

'What made you change?'

'Hitler deserted us,' Paul said. 'He just wrote off the whole Army. He could have saved us, but he didn't.'

'What you are saying, then, is that he was a bad general, a bad tactician, a useless Army leader, and that in the final analysis he let you all down. Is that so, Paul?'

'Yes, you could put it like that.'

'Then,' continued Heide, 'supposing Hitler had not made those mistakes. Supposing he had continued with his successes and gone onto conquer Russia and England—'

'But that didn't happen,' cut in Paul.

'No, thank God, it didn't. But if that had happened, then you soldiers would have gone on praising him?'

Paul said nothing.

Heide looked at him carefully and persisted. 'Did you know about the concentration camps?'

'Yes, I had heard of them.' Paul's' mind was full of the bitter memories of his own captivity. He said, 'You know, the Russian camps were not exactly havens of paradise.'

'Maybe Paul, but remember, they did not start the war.

'No, that's true,' Paul said, 'but the Allies do not realise how fortunate they were not to face the Russians as a foe.'

Heide offered Paul a cigarette, which he took and lit. He inhaled the smoke deeply.

'What was so different about facing the Russians?' asked Heide.

'They came at us in waves. We would destroy them, one after another, but they just came on and on, walking over their dead comrades.'

Heide said nothing for a while and then, 'I know you often thought about Paula. Did you ever think about England and me?'

'Yes,' Paul said, 'especially in the camp. It must have been very hard for you, Uncle. Particularly when I first went back to Germany.' He looked at the old man who had been so kind to him and tried to do so much for him. 'I'm sorry,' he said, and he suddenly broke down and wept. He had not cried for many, many years.

'Can you ever forgive me, Uncle?'

'Of course I forgive you! I love you.' Heide wanted to take Paul in his arms. He wanted to turn back the clock. But he did not move. When Paul recovered they both sat in silence for a long time. Paul was the first to speak.

'You asked me about the concentration camps. I was sometimes told about them and the things going on in them. But most of the time I wasn't prepared to believe the stories.'

'Well, what are your views now, Paul?'

'There is nothing much that I can say. The cruelty in those places seems monstrous and absurd. I've already told you that I've seen so much of death, it has little effect on me.'

Paul stood up and walked over to the window. Heide watched him. Paul wondered if he could ever make his uncle understand. He had fought as a soldier for a country and a leader he had believed in. He turned and looked at his uncle with sad eyes and said, 'I'm very tired. I must sleep.' He moved towards the door, and as he opened it he said, 'There's evil in all of us. We used to talk about things like that in the camp. Some have much more than others. I suppose I have my share of it. It all seems so far away now.'

'What seems far away, Paul?'
'The past.'
'Then it must be the future that is close?'
'Yes – that's right, Uncle – and the future is my son and Paula.'

They stood staring at each other for a moment. Then Paul said, 'I want my son to understand that frontiers must go – countries don't matter – peace matters.'

After Paul had left the room, Heide knew that he could tell Paula to come. Whether they lived in Germany or in England was up to them. He wondered if it would make any difference where they lived.

It was not easy for Heide to arrange a passage for Paula and her son to come to Hamburg. By the time he obtained a booking on a troopship, summer was slipping into autumn. But during this time Paul gained in physical strength. And as his grey-white face took on a healthier tan, Paul's confidence seemed to grow. At last the day came. All morning that day, Paul stayed in his room, alone. He felt exultant. He felt humble. He felt strong. When Heide came in to take him to the docks he quickly went over to his uncle and embraced him. There was no need for words.

Later, at the docks, the two men stood side by side on the quay, watching the troopship slowly approaching. Their eyes searched along its length but they only saw the uniform colour of the soldiers of the British Army. Here and there were the soft blues of some sailors. Heide's face was very white, stone white, as though all the colour had drained from it. Paul saw them first. He saw the woman and the child by her side waving at them. Paul waved back and shouted, 'There! There they are!'

He could see Paula and his son. Never before had he loved them so deeply and so dearly as now. Heide waved with one arm; the other was around Paul's shoulders. Suddenly the tears were running down the old man's cheeks. His life had not been in vain.